FALSE NEGATIVE

FALSE NEGATIVE

DAVID B. RUSTERHOLZ

FALSE NEGATIVE

Cover Art & Internal Layout by Hub70 Design & Print

Dedication

This story is dedicated to all the wonderful undergraduate students that worked on research projects with me throughout my years at UWRF.

Chapter 1   2016, April 5, Tuesday

Unlike so many of her classmates, there were no strategically placed designer rips in the jeans that Lisa Ross wore beneath her white lab coat as she strode down the hallway to the large well-lit room that housed the student research facilities. "Silly and impractical," she would have said, had she been asked. The third floor of the Swensen Science Building at Burlington University in Superior, Wisconsin was devoted entirely to the Chemistry Department and Lisa felt at home in every room here. Now in the spring of her senior year, Lisa had completed all the courses required for her major in chemistry and had taken a number of specialty elective courses as well. Not only had she passed most of her courses with top marks, she had also proposed her own research project and was well on her way to finishing the sequence of chemical reactions that would bring her project to a successful conclusion.

With her light brown ponytail bobbing with every determined step, she entered the laboratory and passed several benches and fume hoods assigned to other students as she proceeded to her own work area. She allowed herself a small feeling of pride as she passed the shelves filled with various chemicals, neatly ordered pieces of esoteric glassware and mysterious instruments. This was her turf. She felt at home here. She knew what all these things were useful for, their different functions, and what they could or could not reveal about a particular chemical's properties. She remembered the occasions when family members had visited her on Parent's Day or Homecoming and she showed them around campus. She could still envision the looks of boredom or bewilderment on their faces when they entered the chemistry labs, clutching their coats a little tighter and asking questions that revealed how little they understood and how little they were really interested. "That's interesting, Lisa," and "Oooh, that looks complicated." But the objects weren't really that complicated, once you understood how they worked and what they did. They were tools. Tools that could do a job, that could provide answers to questions. It was all perfectly logical. And Lisa ruled this domain.

"Lisa?" The voice belonged to Jodi Sanders, a junior chemistry student and friend of Lisa's. Jodi, who at five foot six inches stood the same height as Lisa, had short dark hair that was now squashed into disarray by the band of her safety goggles. Her black leggings and white sneakers protruded below the hem of a somewhat too long white lab coat. Standing in front of her fume hood her goggles reflected the glow of its internal lighting. Inside, a large round-bottomed flask was filled with a swirling golden liquid. Jodi was reading from her notebook, "… piperonal, nitroethane, ammonium nitrate…." She paused. "Lisa? Is this right? I'm sure he said ammonium nitrate."

"Just let me put these down and I'll come see," Lisa called over her shoulder. Lisa proceeded to her desk, set down her books and donned her goggles. Suddenly a bright flash came from the direction of Jodi's hood with a bang that made her ears ring. Stunned, she knelt down and covered her ears as if shielding them now could prevent the concussion that made them sting. As the realization of what had just happened dawned on her, her first concern was for Jodi. Lisa peered over her bench in the direction of Jodi's work area. "Jodi! Jodi!" she called. Lisa hurried to Jodi's hood. Fortunately the safety sash had been down when the explosion occurred; the glass shield was bowing outward severely and was completely spider-webbed. The equipment inside the hood had been reduced to an unrecognizable jumble of metal and glass shards. A viscous odiferous liquid was dripping onto the floor, but fortunately there was no fire. Jodi was lying on the floor and blood was pooling under her head.

"Jodi! Jodi! Are you okay?" Lisa knelt by her side, placed a hand on her shoulder and turned her over far enough to reveal a bleeding wound on her head. The hood sash had saved her from the direct blast of the explosion, but the force had apparently propelled her into the bench across from the hood opening. Lisa peeled off her lab coat and bunched it under Jodi's head. Then she started running for the doorway. The sound of the explosion had been heard by many occupants of the building who were now standing in their doorways looking down the hall. "Come quick!" Lisa called. "Jodi's been hurt." Several students and professors came running and wound their way into the lab room and clustered around Jodi.

"I'm calling an ambulance," said Professor Lydia Martinelli whose office was located closest to the lab. Somebody handed Lisa a paper towel that she applied to Jodi's head. The bleeding seemed to have diminished, but Jodi remained unconscious. Lisa stayed by Jodi's side as students and professors pressed in to look at Jodi and gawk at the damaged fume hood. Some started to mop up the floor around her, scooping up broken glass and soaking up the dripping chemicals. Questions were hurled back and forth. "Is she alive? What was she doing? Did anybody see it happen?" But nobody was offering any answers.

Lisa remained kneeling beside Jodi, adjusting her makeshift pillow and pushing the paper towel against the slowing trickle of blood on her head while the sound of an approaching siren could be heard in the distance. The uniformed EMT attendants arrived and motioned for Lisa to move aside. They performed a brief inspection and then moved Jodi to a stretcher, placed her on a gurney and wheeled her to the elevator and to the waiting ambulance outside.

With Jodi gone and the immediate damage contained, Lisa was joined in the hallway by her research supervisor and department chair, Professor Gerald Barton, who asked Lisa to come to his office. The two of them proceeded down the corridor to where Dr. Barton's office was located.

"Come in. Have a seat. Can I get you something to drink?" Dr. Barton was asking.

"Yes, please." With her ears still ringing faintly, Lisa sat. Realizing that the emergency was over, a rush of exhaustion descended upon her. "Oh my god! Poor Jodi!" she said.

Professor Barton went to his office door and spoke to someone in the next room. A moment later he returned with a coffee mug full of water that he handed to Lisa. He sat down at his desk, but a moment later he rose again to confer with someone who had appeared at his office door. Returning again to his chair, he sat and regarded Lisa as she sipped water from the mug. "Just rest a while, okay?"

After a moment of quiet he spoke again. "The Campus Safety Officer is here and would like to talk with you. Are you up to that?"

"I guess so," she replied vacantly.

Professor Barton went to the door to his office and motioned to someone who had been waiting in his outer office. A portly middle-aged man, slightly balding and sporting a thick mustache, came into the room and introduced himself to Lisa. "I'm Steven Davis, Safety Officer for Burlington U," he began. "I'll need to file a report regarding this accident," he continued, "and I'd like to ask you a few questions. Alright?"

Lisa agreed while Professor Barton stood, waiting in the doorway.

"So, first of all, what were you doing in the room?"

"I had just gotten there. I was putting my books down at my bench when the explosion occurred."

"Lisa works for me," Barton interjected. "Her bench is in the third bay from the door."

Davis nodded and continued. "And what was Miss Sanders doing?"

"She was running a reaction," said Lisa. "She works for Dr. Rathburn. I know that it is mainly organic synthesis. But I don't know any specifics. He has a grant from SynZac. He prepares intermediates for them."

"So, you have no idea what chemicals Jodi was working with?"

Lisa tried to remember what Jodi had said just before the explosion. "No, well… no, not really. She had just asked me to come and check something in her notebook. She had a question about it." Lisa struggled to recall what Jodi had said but the excitement of the day was blurring her memory. "I'm sorry. I can't remember for sure. But you could look in her notebook. It should all be there."

"Yes," agreed Davis. "We'll check." He sat back and studied Lisa for a moment. "If you happen to remember anything that she said about what she was working with, I want you to come and tell me right away, okay?"

"Okay," Lisa agreed, "but I…"

Davis cut her off and stood to leave. "Oh, and you should stop by Campus Health. It wouldn't hurt to have them check you over, too. Make sure everything is okay. Alright?"

"Okay." Lisa nodded in agreement, then said, "What about Jodi? Is she okay?"

"The last I heard is that they took her to Memorial Hospital. I don't really know anything more."

"Has anybody told her roommates? Do her parents know?"

Davis nodded. "I will be calling her parents next. As soon as I talk to the hospital. Do you know who her roommates are? I can contact them, or you can, if you want."

"Yeah. Her roommates are Jordan Lewis and Abby Decker. They live in a house off campus; I'm not sure where exactly. You contact them, please," said Lisa. "I really don't feel up to it right now."

"Oh, by the way," said Barton, "I believe that Andy Treydon is waiting out in the hall. Would it be okay if he walked you over to Campus Health?"

"Oh, that'd be fine," responded Lisa. Like Lisa, Andy Treydon was a senior, majoring in Chemistry at Burlington, who also did research under the direction of Professor Barton. Lisa and Andy had taken many of their courses together and gradually had become friends. During the past year the friendship had grown into something a bit stronger. There was a mutual admiration and respect between them, but more recently they had come to acknowledge an attraction that went beyond the simple comfort that they felt in each other's presence.

They all got to their feet and moved into Barton's outer office where they found Professor Rathburn pacing nervously. "Gerald, I've got to talk to you," Rathburn blurted.

"I'll be with you in a minute, Charles," said Barton holding up his hand. Stepping into the hallway, Barton and Lisa found a young man with dark hair wearing jeans and a plaid flannel shirt.

Andy greeted Lisa gently as she stepped into the hall. "Hey, Lis. How're you doing?"

"Not great," she replied. "My ears are still ringing, and I just can't stop worrying about Jodi."

"Yeah," Andy agreed. "I wonder what caused the explosion. Do you have any idea?"

"Not really. I wish I could remember. Right before it happened she asked me to check something in her notebook, but I went to my desk first and then,

then… it was so loud," she trailed off.

The two collected Lisa's books and backpack and walked south across campus to the Student Health Center in the lower level of one of the dormitories. Andy sat on an uncomfortable plastic chair and waited in a small lounge while Lisa talked to the on-duty nurse. After a short interview and a superficial examination of her ears, Lisa was released. The two quietly walked the four blocks to Lisa's off-campus apartment. At her doorway Andy wrapped his arms around her. "I'm sure am glad that you're okay."

Lisa leaned her head against his chest feeling the weight of exhaustion and the gravity of the events of the afternoon. "Thank you, Andy." She turned her face up to his and kissed him briefly.

"I'll see you tomorrow, okay?" he asked.

Lisa understood that Andy was referring to an afternoon study date they shared on a regular basis. "Yeah, see you tomorrow."

Andy watched as Lisa waved and went inside. Then he turned and walked the several blocks toward his own apartment. The growing dusk and a loneliness that was all too familiar set him thinking, thinking about Lisa. It was unfamiliar for him to see Lisa so shaken. She always seemed so confident and strong to him. Andy wished that he could have such confidence. He had a pretty good idea of what he wanted to do with his life; he wanted to be a scientist. Chemistry, physics, biology, it was all interesting. Exciting things were being discovered. Cool machines were being created, and he wanted to be a part of it all. He had gotten good grades in high school and with a little studying he had been doing well in his college courses. But how to get to where he wanted to be in the future was unknown to him. How is it that Lisa seemed to know her forward path so well? He felt happy when Lisa was around. She was so pretty, her soft brown shoulder length hair, her impish smile. It made him think about doing things that had nothing to do with science, well, maybe biology. But what did she see in him? Anything? Why would she care about him? She seemed to know exactly where she was going. Would her plans possibly include the likes of Andy? Does she even think that he will be in her future?

Andy tried to imagine himself and Lisa as a married couple, and immediately he was confronted by the contrast that he knew existed between their families. Lisa came from a well-to-do family in St. Paul, Minnesota where her father was a member of a large, respected law firm. Lisa had two older sisters, one who had become a lawyer somewhere on the East Coast, and the other who was currently in graduate school in economics in Arizona somewhere. On the other hand, Andy had grown up in the rural town of St. Croix Falls, Wisconsin. He had been an only child, raised primarily by his mother after his dad had disappeared when he was eight years old. Having lived on the outskirts of town, Andy had few opportunities to hang out with other kids his age and had found ways to keep himself entertained alone. He read books and amassed bug, rock, and plant collections. He tried to find ways to conduct science experiments with whatever simple apparatus he could get his hands on. His wide reading and good study habits afforded him success in school, but he wished for companionship and affection. Andy's mother had always been a supportive influence, buying books and inexpensive toys, tools and equipment that fostered his curiosity. In particular, Andy's involvement with the local Boy Scout Troop had been a positive experience. He enjoyed participating in physical activities with other boys, although he found that he was not a leader. He was also gratified to learn that it was easy for him to master the various skills that were taught, and he gained a confidence that, at least in the outdoors, he could rely on himself for basic survival.

Dealing with people, however, was more complicated. Andy wanted to be liked but was unsure what the social rules were. The previous fall, at the event called Parent's Day that doubled as Homecoming on the Burlington campus, when many alumni and families came to visit, Lisa had introduced Andy to her parents. Andy remembered Lisa's mother asking, "So, Andy, what does your father do?"

"I don't have a father," he had replied. "My mother's a nurse in a hospital in St. Croix Falls."

"Oh, I see," she had replied. But there were no more questions, and Andy had felt that as a subject he had suddenly become very uninteresting.

"Right," he thought as he turned from the sidewalk to the entrance into his apartment building. Thoughts of Lisa dissipated as thoughts of pizza and how he was going to attack his evening studies flooded in.

Chapter 2   2013, October 4, Friday

Cynthia Collins thought that her meeting with Professor Rathburn had gone just perfectly. Although a few moments ago she was in the rather compromising position of being bent over his desk with her lacy red panties around her ankles and her skirt bunched around her waist, she felt confident that her grade on the up-coming organic chemistry mid-term was going to be quite satisfactory. Besides, the event had not been without a degree of pleasure for her, too.

Earlier that afternoon Cynthia had considered her reflection in the bathroom mirror of her off-campus apartment and thought about how much she looked like her mother. The resemblance was quite noticeable, but that was okay. Her mother was a strong confident woman. Although she was unsure of exactly what events might transpire during her meeting with Professor Rathburn, Cynthia had prepared by washing and putting a gentle curl into her long black hair and applying a touch of perfume to some of her more intimate areas. In high school, she had become enamored for a time with Goth styles of dress and appearance, but she had largely abandoned these when she started college. Still, she sported black nail polish and favored a strong application of dark eye shadow. Although skirts were hardly ever worn by the female students these days, she knew what appealed to men, and so had selected a skirt and blouse combination that would facilitate the events that she thought might develop.

She had also considered when the best time to approach Professor Rathburn would be. Late on a Friday afternoon would be good. The building would be emptying out as commuters left for the weekend and even the on-campus students would be heading away for local entertainment.

Climbing the stairs to the third floor of the Science Building, Cynthia pressed her fingers momentarily to the reassuring lump of implanted birth control inside her left arm. "Ready," she thought. A vision of her mother came back to her, sitting at the foot of her bed one night when she had come home from an unhappy incident with a boyfriend in high school. "Men will use you in this world if you let them," she had said. "Just don't let them. Figure out what you want and go for that. Make sure that you are the one who's in control. Letting some boy get you pregnant is a sure way to become a victim. Stay safe. If trouble is coming, get out. Before it's too late. Don't forget." Cynthia hadn't forgotten.

Having grown up on the north side of Chicago, Cynthia had met a variety of people in her youth and had been exposed to a variety of worldly ways. Her parents had divorced shortly after she was born, and although she had amicable meetings with her father on occasion, she was mostly raised by her mother who had a steady full-time job as a seamstress. Home life was generally pleasant and without conflict. As Cynthia aged through middle school and high school, her friends had educated her in some of the less reputable forms of entertainment. She had sampled cigarettes, marijuana and alcohol, and though none of these held a strong attraction for her, she didn't hesitate to enjoy them whenever the occasion arose. Her first forays into sexual encounters had been with boys her own age, and these had been generally uninspiring. However, she learned that sex seemed to have a very strong influence on the average male, and she became quite aware that if she used it judiciously, she could manipulate some people and events to her advantage.

In high school, Cynthia found that she was naturally smart enough that academic success came without much work on her part. Happily, she discovered that many of her courses were, in fact, interesting, and with minimal effort she was able to earn good grades. It all seemed more sensible than rebelling. She had loosely decided that as a career choice some area of science would be most interesting. She had seen pharmacists in her local drug stores and thought that pharmacy looked like an attractive profession. As a result, she had registered for the pre-pharmacy curriculum when she arrived at Burlington. The first-year science courses were largely a review of topics that she had learned in high school, but her second-year course in organic chemistry taught by Professor Rathburn proved to be a more serious challenge. The need to spend longer hours with the textbook coupled with a fear of failing to meet the required standards for admission to professional school prompted her to consider alternative methods for assuring a good grade in his course. Thus, as the first major mid-term exam loomed, she felt the need to appeal to the instructor in a way that would boost her confidence for success in his course.

For his part, Charles Rathburn was rather attractive in a British sort of way. He was of medium height and weight, with dark hair that was starting to recede. His dressing habits were always neat and stylish and usually included a tweed sport jacket with soft leather patches at the elbows. He spoke with a faint East-coast accent and pronounced his words with precision and delicacy. Although he presented himself with a no-nonsense demeanor, Cynthia had suspected, correctly, that beneath his officious exterior there lurked the natural urges of a healthy heterosexual male. More than once she had caught him watching her and some of the other young women in his class. She had returned his gaze with a smile, and she could tell that he was interested in a way that had little to do with the words on the textbook's page.

The event that Cynthia suspected was coming had been brewing for several weeks. Since the first day of the fall semester classes, Cynthia was aware that Professor Rathburn had a special interest in her. More than once she had looked up in class to find him watching her. In the lab class, he would always make a point to come to her station and spend a little extra time checking her work, and occasionally placing a hand on her shoulder when he spoke to her. She always received a smile and a greeting when they would meet in the hallway. Now, walking the corridor towards Rathburn's office, she thought about her mother's advice. "Yeah. What do I want? What does he want? And who's in control?" She knew what she wanted, and she was pretty sure that she knew what Professor Rathburn wanted. "I guess we'll see just who is in control of what," she mused.

Cynthia knocked gently on Rathburn's door. "Come in," came the brusque response. She entered to find the professor sitting at his desk with a pile of papers before him. His horn-rimmed glasses were perched far down on his nose and a red pen was wavering in his fingers ready to pounce on whatever error was going to be found next. "Yes…?" he said, barely looking at her.

"Hi," she began, "I'm Cynthia. Cynthia Collins. I'm in your ten o'clock organic lecture."

"Oh, hello," he greeted her, recognition dawning. He set his pen down and swiveled his chair to face her. "Oh this little chickie," he thought. "What a treat to have her stop by." Then, in a more polite tone he said, "Come in, come in."

Cynthia looked around the small office. The window beside the desk that normally would have had a pleasant view of the campus mall, was now covered by a heavy curtain. The rest of the walls were floor-to-ceiling bookshelves filled with heavy tomes, bound journals, three-ring binders, and stacked manila folders. Prominently displayed over his desk was a framed diploma and a couple of black and white photographs showing Professor Rathburn shaking hands with some unknown dignitaries. A large computer monitor sat to one side. Making an obvious display of admiring her surroundings, Cynthia moved to Rathburn's desk and leaned to examine the photographs. In doing so her blouse was stretched tightly over her chest and positioned directly in Rathburn's view. "Who are these people?" she asked, indicating the photographs.

"Oh, just some people that you probably wouldn't know," replied Rathburn slowly as he took some time to admire the swell of Cynthia's breasts. Regaining his composure, Rathburn continued, "Please, sit down." Cynthia sat in the chair beside his desk, set her backpack on the floor at her feet and adjusted the hem of her skirt that barely reached her knees while Rathburn continued to admire her. "So, Miss Collins, I must say that you are looking particularly lovely this evening. Tell me, what brings you to my door?"

Cynthia smiled and leaned over to pull a spiral notebook from her backpack. "Well, a couple things," she replied. "First of all, I'm wondering whether you can help me understand that R and S business in stereochemistry. And then, well, I'm here because I'm worried about the exam next week and my grade in your class." She flipped open her notebook.

"Well, yes, um, let's see," said Rathburn finally taking his eyes off Cynthia and turning his attention to his computer monitor. After typing a few strokes, he sat back and said, "Yes, I can see that you have quite a bit of room for improvement."

"Yes, well, that's why I'm here," she said meekly, looking down at her lap. "I was wondering whether you could give me some advice. I've been studying harder in this class than I ever have in any other class." She hoped that she'd put just the right amount of pleading into her voice.

Rathburn sat, considering this very attractive and submissive young woman in front of him. Was she making a play for him? He wasn't sure, but it was flattering to think that she was. Although he knew that he should send her packing to the library, her sexual appeal was undeniable. "How far is she willing to take this?" he wondered. "Well, Cynthia," he began, enjoying the titillation of the whole situation and wishing to prolong it, "let's begin here." Rathburn sorted through several papers on his desk and pulled out one that was labeled Stereochemistry Worksheet. "Here's the problem set that we did last week. Why don't you show me how you would work through these." Cynthia shifted her chair a little closer so that the two of them were sitting side by side. Writing slowly on the page, she described how she would approach each of the problems while Rathburn looked on and provided prompts and comments at various stages. Sitting close together with their arms touching occasionally, Rathburn could smell Cynthia's perfume and was acutely aware of her physical presence. At one point, Rathburn brought out some plastic molecular models that they handled together, their hands momentarily touching as they worked with them together.

"You make it look so easy, Dr. Rathburn," commented Cynthia.

"Thanks. But I've been at it for a while. You keep practicing. I think that you're getting the hang of it now," he replied.

As they came to the end of the worksheet, Cynthia sat back. "Wow, that really helps. I think I get it now." She closed her notebook and put it back into her backpack. "Can you tell me how I'm doing in your class so far? Is there any chance that I will be able to get an A? You know that my major is pre-pharmacy and I've got to have really good science grades to get in."

Rathburn wiggled his computer mouse and a spreadsheet appeared on his screen. "Well, Cynthia," he began, "so far your scores have not been outstanding. It looks like you're performing at the C level. You are going to have to get some good scores on the next tests and quizzes if you're going to bring that up."

Cynthia looked down at her hands clasped in her lap. "Well, uh, sir, I was wondering, uh thinking, uh, do you think there is something that I could do for extra credit?" She shifted in her chair sitting a bit closer to his so their knees were touching.

Charles felt his arousal growing and his will to resist failing. "Yes, I think this young woman is really making herself available to me," he thought. His heart was starting to pound in his chest. He reached for Cynthia's hand and took it so that they were holding hands in her lap. His face was close to hers; her hair and her perfume were so bewitching. "It would take me a lot of time to create a special worksheet just for you," he said. "We would have to think of something else."

"Oh, Dr. Rathburn," Cynthia said shyly, gently rubbing his hand. The movement of their hands together in her lap was causing the hem of her skirt to ride higher on her thighs. She moved her hand that was not occupied with his to rest on his thigh. "I hope that we can think of something. I really do need a good grade in your class." She raised her face to give him her most pleading look.

A little while later Cynthia stepped into the hallway gently closing Rathburn's door behind her. Looking left and right she was pleased to see that the corridor was nearly empty. A lone figure sat on a bench at the end of the hall. Cynthia turned and proceeded to the stairs in the opposite direction. "Yes, that went very well," she thought. It was particularly pleasing that upon parting, Rathburn had indicated that he might be open to a repeat performance at some future date. "He actually was kind of a gentleman," she thought, smiling to herself. "I could see this going on for a while." Remembering her mother's advice, she thought about getting Rathburn to use a condom. Birth control wasn't the only issue here, there were STDs to think about, too. It had become clear this afternoon that this guy wasn't inexperienced, and she didn't need any extra trouble. He had responded nicely to her today. "Set the hook, and reel him in. He'll wear one," she thought confidently. She'd brought along a few guys in her past who were more resistant than Charles Rathburn would likely be.

As she descended the stairs, her thoughts turned to where she was going next, which brought to mind her off campus apartment and her current boyfriend, Peter Dahle. Shaking her head slightly, she thought, "No. There is no reason Peter needs to know about any of this."

⚗

Earlier that afternoon, Steven Davis, the senior Campus Safety Officer had placed his phone receiver back in its cradle with a little more vigor than might have been good for it. "That guy is going to get the worst assignments from now on," he thought. "Calling in sick on a Friday afternoon! How does he think I am going to get anybody to cover for his shift tonight?" Davis reached for the schedule book to check exactly on the list of duties the absent night officer was supposed to have covered. "Damn!" he thought again to himself as he realized all the tasks that he would be doing while he worked a second shift. Davis, who was slightly overweight, out-of-shape, and definitely not fond of physical work, saw that he would be making rounds through every building on campus, checking to see that doors were locked, lights were turned off, and everything left in secure condition for the weekend. "Oh, blast!" he muttered as he hoisted his bulk from his chair. Although many students would remain on campus throughout the weekend, and a few professors would still be working in their offices late on a Friday, Davis decided to get started on his trek. The sooner he completed the circuit, the sooner he could go back to his office and sit. If somebody was still working and unlocked a door that he had already locked, he didn't really care. It's not like the campus was a high crime area. They had their share of petty thefts and senseless college pranks. But it was rare that there were any serious crimes. Perhaps the biggest problem was the underage drinking. Almost every other weekend, some young person was found bent over and throwing up beside one of the campus walkways, and once in a while some student would need a trip to the ER. Infractions that happened off campus were handled by the Superior Police Department. Either way, violators were subject to a significant fine and repeat offenders faced possible expulsion from the campus. There was probably a fair amount of illegal drug use in the dorms and off campus, but it was rarely serious enough to provoke the attention of the police. Nevertheless, the circuit of the campus buildings had to be made, and he might as well get it over with.

An hour later Davis was still in the middle of his rounds. He had entered the south end of the Swensen Science Building, toured the ground floor, which was occupied by the Physics Department, came back through the second floor, which contained Biology, and now had climbed to the third floor where the Chemistry Department's offices, laboratories, and classrooms held residence. The first door that he encountered was unlocked and led into a laboratory. A few of its lights had been left on, so Davis went in to investigate. He passed by racks of odd-shaped pieces of glassware, and shelves containing bottles with names that he had no idea how to pronounce. "What is all of this stuff?" he wondered. "What does it do?" Having no real understanding of chemistry, his imagination led him to scenes that he had seen in sci-fi movies and crime dramas. Pushing aside thoughts of deadly poisons and caustic liquids, he retreated to the doorway, turned off the lights and locked the door.

Farther down the hall, he observed a glow coming from under the door to one of the professors' offices. He stopped outside the door and read the nameplate. "Looks like Professor Charles Rathburn is working late," he thought. He was about to knock before using his master key, when he heard sounds coming from within. Clearly there were two people inside, and one had a much higher voice than the other. It was also clear that they weren't talking, unless they were communicating using a variety of inarticulate moans and gasps. "Hmmm..." he thought with his hand poised in mid-air. Instead of knocking, he ambled a distance back down the hall to a bench where he sat and waited quietly. Sure enough, about ten minutes later, a young woman with dark hair emerged and walked toward the stairwell at the far end of the building.

Chapter 3   2016, April 5, Tuesday

Jordan Lewis and Abby Decker chained their bicycles to the metal railing at the side of the house and clomped up the stairs to their third floor off-campus apartment in the 1400 block of Hammond Ave. Like many student apartments in the area, it had been carved out of a large clapboard-sided 1920s era house that was showing its age and a degree of neglect by the landlord. The furnishings were minimal. A white patterned Formica and metal table with three matching chairs were crowded into a small kitchen. The living room featured a broken-down couch, one over-stuffed chair, and a coffee table. A single poster advertising a concert by a bygone rock band adorned one wall. The only modern touches were a large flat-screen TV against one wall across from the couch and a couple of Blue-Tooth speakers. The window shades at one end of the room were non-functional. There were some thin drapes, but the view from the windows was only into the upper branches of the trees on the boulevard, so the drapes were not necessary and rarely, if ever, closed. The coffee table was littered with empty pop cans, some pens, a few crumpled sheets of paper and an ashtray that was in need of emptying.

In a general studies psychology course during their freshman year two years earlier, Jordan, an economics and business major, had become friends with Abby, an elementary education major, and Jodi Sanders, a chemistry major. Abby and Jodi had initially been assigned as roommates in the dorm and that had gone well. They tended to keep similar hours, shared similar standards of cleanliness, were respectful of each other's space and liked the same music. So this year the three had opted to rent off-campus accommodations, and Jordan, who had become Abby's boyfriend, was happy for the live-in arrangement. The fact that Jodi's chosen major meant that she spent long hours away from the apartment, studying and working in the lab, was just fine with Abby and Jordan.

Jordan and Abby dumped their books and coats in their respective bedrooms that both had mattresses laid directly on the floor and storage boxes for furniture. Back in the kitchen they examined the contents of the refrigerator, pulled out a frozen pizza, turned on the oven and each grabbed a can of soda before flopping on the couch. "Is Jodi here?" asked Jordan.

"Nah," replied Abby.

"Ah! In that case," said Jordan, setting down his can, "I'm going to light one of these." He pulled a hand-rolled cigarette from his shirt pocket and held it up for Abby to see.

"All right," said Abby with enthusiasm.

Jordan pulled a Bic lighter from his pocket, lit the joint and inhaled deeply. They passed it back and forth until they'd had enough and put it out. Leaning back lazily into the couch, Jordan pulled out his cellphone and punched a few buttons. Soon soft music was emanating from the speakers around the room. Abby closed her eyes, hummed along and smiled.

Rousing somewhat from her relaxed state, Abby regarded Jordan. "I've got nothing due for a day or two. How about you?"

"Same here," said Jordan dreamily.

"And who knows when Jodi will get back …"

"Yeah? What are you thinking?"

"Well, it's just you and me, and …." she paused, "… and a little X."

Jordan sat up. "You've got some Ecstasy?"

"Yeah. Ya wanna do it?" Abby said smiling mischievously. "Ya wanna do it with me?" she said emphasizing the last two words. Now she was grinning at him.

"You bet your baby blue socks, babe," said Jordan. "Let's go."

Abby went to her room and came back holding a couple of bicolored capsules in her hand. Jordan stood to meet her. They each took a capsule, swallowed it and followed with a sip of soda. Smiling at each other, they embraced and kissed. After several seconds of hugging and kissing they held hands and sat on the couch. "We'll get to more of that later," said Abby with a meaningful glance.

"Where did you get it?" asked Jordan.

Abby looked sideways at Jordan. "I could tell you, but then I'd have to shoot you."

"Okay," said Jordan, shifting his gaze away from her, "shoot me."

"No, really," said Abby. "But you have to keep it a secret. Okay?"

"No problem," said Jordan.

"Do you know Peter Dahle?" she began. "I met him in a psych class freshman year. He seems to know where to get it. I see him occasionally."

"Oh yeah. Is he the guy that's going with that Cynthia girl, the one with the dark hair?"

"Yup. That's the one."

Jordan nodded, "Okay then. Mum's the word."

The oven timer buzzed indicating that it was up to the set temperature, so Jordan rose to put the pizza in. He returned with his hand held out to her, motioning for her to get up. For a few steps they danced and swayed with the music. Feeling the Ecstasy, the two closed their eyes and danced close together. When the song ended, Jordan punched some more buttons on his phone and soon a faster up-beat tune was playing. Their dancing became more animated, gyrating and laughing as they reveled in the growing sensations until the timer buzzed again signaling the readiness of their pizza.

They were sitting at the kitchen table gingerly nibbling at the hot pizza when Abby's phone rang. She picked it up and looked at the caller ID screen. "Unknown caller," it read.

"I dunno," she muttered, and then, "It's a local number, I guess…" She punched "Accept."

Jordan overheard Abby's end of the conversation as she stood and walked into the living room. "Yes, … yes… What! … Oh my God, no! …. How? …." There was a long silence. Then, "Sure… okay, … yeah. Thanks for calling. Bye."

Abby lowered her phone and slowly turned to Jordan with a look of shock on her face. "That was a Mr. Davis from the Burlington Campus Safety office or something," she began. "Jodi has been in some kind of accident in the chem lab. She won't be coming back tonight. She is in the hospital." Abby moved to the couch and sat hunched forward as she digested the meaning of what she had just heard. "Oh my gosh! Poor Jodi. I wonder if she will be okay? What should we do?"

Jordan stood and came over to Abby. "I don't know…" he began. "What can we do?" He gazed around the room as if an answer could be found there. The rhythmic music emanating from the speakers and the drug in his brain that usually accompanied pleasurable excitement made it hard to focus on the seriousness of the news they had just received.

"Should we go see her?" Abby asked.

"I don't think that we should go anywhere right now," said Jordan grimly. "And besides, what good would we be if she's lying in some hospital bed?"

"Yeah, I guess you're right. Oh, I hope she'll be okay."

They sat on the couch and Jordan put his arm around Abby's shoulder. The two sat thinking and trying to focus. Finally Jordan spoke, "I guess we'll just have to wait and find out more later, okay? Let's finish the pizza now before it gets cold. Tomorrow we'll find out if there is something that we can do to help. Alright?"

Chapter 4   2016, April 6, Wednesday

The next morning at 10:55 a.m., Andy entered the anteroom to Dr. Gerald Barton's office and greeted the departmental administrative assistant, "Good morning, Mrs. Barnes."

"Good morning to you, too," she replied cheerfully. "Dr. Barton is with Dr. Rathburn at the moment, but I expect they will be done soon."

Andy nodded and sat in the one available chair, his notebook on his lap. The open door to Dr. Barton's office made the conversation inside easily overheard. "She was working under your supervision," Dr. Barton was saying, "so you're in charge of this investigation. You and Mr. Davis. But the rest of us are all waiting for some reasonable explanation for why the explosion occurred. Good grief! Your excuse that what you do for SynZac is confidential is wearing a little thin right now. The president, the trustees, not to mention the parents, by God, everybody wants to know. We've got a student unconscious in the hospital. The insurance investigators are going to be here tomorrow. So, have your report ready by then. Got it? Good grief."

Following a muffled reply Professor Rathburn appeared, scowled at Andy and Mrs. Barnes, and hurriedly exited through the outer office. Dr. Barton appeared in the doorway. With a friendlier tone than what Andy had just overheard, he greeted Andy with a smile, "Hey Andy, Come on in."

The office accorded the Chairman of the Chemistry Department at Burlington University was barely adequate for any person who had the responsibilities of managing the departmental personnel, overseeing the yearly budget, reporting to the college dean, teaching an only slightly reduced load compared to other faculty, acting as public persona for the occasional visiting dignitary, and maintaining an active research program. The one consolation that set Dr. Barton's office apart from the others was an attached outer office that was occupied by an administrative assistant, Miriam Barnes, who handled much of the record-keeping, fielded phone calls, and was the front line of defense against students who kept finding ways to circumvent the rules that had been developed to guide them successfully through their academic careers.

Gerald Barton was a popular chairman. At 6'2" with broad shoulders and dark hair that showed no sign of thinning, he presented a commanding figure. Although much more casual dress had become the norm for faculty around the campus, Barton regularly wore a shirt and tie combination covered by a sport coat. He had little interest in campus politics, but still tried to keep the faculty under his jurisdiction happy. He looked for ways to compromise and build consensus, and the faculty under him recognized his sincerity. As a result, the department remained a congenial place for faculty and students alike.

Dr. Barton sat down in a comfortable looking swivel chair, pushed aside an open notebook he had been working on, and pulled a folder from a stack to one side of his desk. Andy sat and looked around the small room. Two of the walls were covered by floor to ceiling bookcases filled with significant-looking books. Two of the shelves were filled with volumes of journals all bound with the same-colored covers. File cabinets filled another wall, which then left room for only one additional chair alongside the one occupied by Dr. Barton. Opening a file folder with Andy's name on the tab, Dr. Barton flipped it open and glanced at the top page. Adjusting the glasses on his nose, he looked at Andy and asked, "So. How did that last reaction go?"

"Well. Pretty well, I'd say, but not as good as we'd like." Andy flipped his notebook open and scanned his notes. "After mixing the reactants at zero degrees, I let it warm to room temperature and then stir overnight. The reaction time was about sixteen hours. After work-up I got only about a sixty-five percent isolated yield. That's after one recrystallization. So, not bad, but probably not as good as we'd like."

"Hmmm," commented Barton. "What was the catalyst ratio?"

"Five percent," replied Andy.

The two continued to discuss the conditions of the reaction that Andy was trying to perform as part of his research project, with Barton making suggestions and Andy taking notes. As a senior student majoring in chemistry, that previous fall Andy had jumped at the opportunity to work with Barton. Andy had taken a sophomore course with him and really liked and respected Dr. Barton's authoritative stature coupled with his friendly easy-going demeanor. In return, Barton demonstrated a fatherly concern for Andy that was comforting and confidence-building.

As their discussion wound down, Andy closed his notebook and prepared to leave. Barton leaned back and regarded Andy for a moment. "Andy, do you know what you will be doing next year?"

"I'm not entirely sure, sir," he replied. "As you know, I took the GRE last fall, and I sent in an application to the U of M in Minneapolis, for which you wrote me a letter of recommendation, but so far they have only told me that I'm on a waiting list."

"Hmmm, I'm surprised that you haven't been admitted. You've got good grades, and I know my letter was positive." Barton thought for a moment. "Has anybody talked to you about other options?"

"No, not really."

"Well, graduate school is a great choice, but you also could go straight into industry. That's a good road, too. If you enjoy the technical work, you'd get a lot of experience. It's a very interesting and rewarding pathway."

"That sounds good, sir. I really do enjoy the bench work."

"Yes, well, keep your options open, if you can. Anyway, here's the thing. There's a job fair coming up in a week or so down at the Minneapolis Convention Center. You should go and check out the different possibilities. And remember, whatever you apply for, be sure to ask me for a letter. I think that you have definitely got what it takes to succeed at whatever you choose. You've got the intelligence, research experience, and, I think, a good sense for experimental design. So, be sure to let me know where you decide to apply, okay?"

"Thank you very much, Dr. Barton. You'll definitely be hearing from me. Thank you!" Andy rose and pushed his chair back.

"Alright. I'll see you later. Let me know when you've run that next reaction." Barton smiled and turned back to his desk as Andy departed. Heading toward the student assistants' lounge, Andy clutched his notebook. The success of his project and support of Dr. Barton filled him with an excitement that he was not used to. "Yeah. Maybe I can do this," he thought.

Later that afternoon, Andy joined Lisa on the steps of The Hansen-Torgerson Memorial Library on the Burlington University campus. There was no need for the "Quiet!" sign posted inside the main hall. The size and grandeur of the room was enough to command a hush of awe and respect from all who entered. The stately pillared building had been funded in the early days of the University by a gift from two donors who wanted to be remembered for their dedication to scholarship. Inside, the main hall was open to three stories ringed by balconies. Stacks of books filled the shelves on every level accessed by rolling ladders that children would never be allowed to play on. The floor was filled with long massive oak tables illuminated by green glass shaded lamps. The air fairly breathed, "Here is knowledge, gleaned from the ages. Read, and you will learn."

When electronic files began to replace printed media, the school adapted by constructing a new wing to the library that housed a computer center, the Department of Digital Technology Services and a variety of special classrooms designed to keep pace with students' expectations for entertainment on a wide screen. Unfortunately, the new wing could not be built in a style that adequately matched the brown rusticated stone of the original building. So, although the University had kept pace with the demands of the times, the grandeur of the original building was rather lessened by the new addition.

Lisa and Andy enjoyed meeting for study sessions in the great hall. It was not a place for conversation. Rather, they both valued the effect that the hall had upon their studies. It helped them to believe that their dedication to learning was somehow noble. And they enjoyed knowing that there was another person who shared their secret little pleasure.

At two o'clock they had met on the steps, gone inside and spread their books on their favorite table. It wasn't long until Lisa looked up in exasperation. "Andy, I've got to talk to you."

Andy regarded her for a moment, checked the time on his phone and looked forlornly at his notebook. "Okay," he agreed and gathered his belongings into his backpack.

Across the tree-lined mall from the library was the large modern University Student Center that housed the main food service cafeteria, a smaller fast-food cafeteria, a bookstore, meeting rooms, a small theater, a small auditorium where musical groups sometimes performed, a recreational area with pool and ping-pong tables, and a variety of nooks and crannies filled with lounge chairs and coffee tables. Lisa and Andy found their way to the coffee shop and charged a couple of lattes to their cards. After settling into a private booth, Lisa studied the cup in her hands. "I wish I could remember what it was that Jodi was trying to ask me about. It just keeps nagging at me. If only I had looked at that sooner, maybe I could have prevented the accident."

"On the other hand," Andy responded, "I'm glad you weren't standing next to her when it went off."

"Yeah, true." She shook her head. "I wonder how she is doing. Do you think we could visit her in the hospital?"

"I don't see why not. Let me check on their visiting hours." Andy picked up his cellphone and located the necessary information. "We could go right now if you want. Visiting hours go until 8 p.m."

Minutes later Andy and Lisa were riding up South Tower Avenue in Andy's somewhat battered 2002 green Ford Escort. Memorial Hospital was located in an area that at one time had been the site of a busy commercial hub, but today it was bleaker and lonelier. Many businesses had gone under with the advent of modern internet retailing. Abandoned, boarded up store fronts, dilapidated houses in need of paint, and fenced yards with nonsensical accumulations of junk lined the street.

Eventually the hospital came into view. In contrast to the appearance of the surrounding neighborhood, the hospital budget still allowed for maintenance of its building and grounds. A graceful circular drive led to a large parking lot. Visitors were welcomed by signs that directed them to several different entrances. Sidewalks crisscrossed the neatly mowed lawns bedecked with stately oak trees and occasional benches and picnic tables. Andy parked his car, and they went inside. The reception area was brightly lit and sparsely decorated with uncomfortable-looking chairs, a few large potted plants and an assortment of uninteresting magazines. The receptionist gave them the room number and pointed them in the direction of the elevators. Minutes later they were traversing the fifth floor looking for Jodi's room. Andy sniffed the air and looked at Lisa who did the same.

"Smells like isopropyl alcohol," he said.

"You mean isopropanol?" she replied.

"No, I think it's 2-propanol."

They smiled, enjoying this small moment of shared appreciation of their chemical knowledge.

When they arrived at Jodi's room, they found her door partly open, and they could see a middle-aged couple sitting beside a bed upon which their friend was lying, eyes closed, a tube in her arm and various instruments with glowing numbers and winking lights behind the head of her bed.

Andy knocked gently. "Hello," he called. The man and the woman arose. "Hello," he said again and advanced into the room. "I'm Andy Treydon and this is Lisa Ross. We're friends of Jodi's."

"Hello, come on in," the man said. "I'm Don Sanders and this is my wife, Linda. We're Jodi's parents." The couple looked tired, as if they had been up all night. Their somber expressions, rumpled clothing and slightly mussed hair testified to their heartfelt concern for their daughter's well-being.

Lying under a blanket on the bed, what was visible of Jodi's body appeared to be intact. A small bandage was wrapped around her head. There were no other apparent injuries. Lisa stepped to the side of the bed. "How is she?" she asked.

Mrs. Sanders wrung her hands and answered, "The doctors think that she is going to be okay, they say. She apparently struck her head pretty hard when she fell. They think that she could wake up anytime, but they just don't know. They're talking about doing an MRI if she doesn't wake up soon."

"I'm so sorry," commented Lisa. Andy stood nodding in agreement.

"Do you know how it happened?" Jodi's father asked.

"Not exactly," said Lisa. "I was in the room at the time. Jodi had just asked me to check something in her notebook, but I went to my desk to set my books down first. I'm really frustrated that I can't remember what she asked me when I came in."

"Jodi's project was under the supervision of Professor Rathburn. He should be able to tell us what she was doing," volunteered Andy.

They all considered this in silence for a minute while looking at Jodi.

"Have you met Professor Rathburn?" asked Lisa, trying to keep the conversation going.

Don and Linda looked at each other. "No, I don't think that we've ever met him," replied Linda. "There was a Mr. Davis here from Burlington. He was the one who called us. I think he said he was from the Campus Safety Department or something. He seemed real nice."

The four stood around Jodi's bed as the conversation lagged. "So, were you and Jodi in some of the same classes?" asked Linda.

"No," responded Lisa, "we're a year ahead of Jodi, but we work in the same research lab, and she has a desk in the assistants' room where we have desks." She nodded in Andy's direction. "So, we see her all the time and just hang out together."

Linda nodded. "Where are you all from?"

"I'm from St. Croix Falls," replied Andy, "Lisa's from St. Paul."

"Do you like Burlington?"

"Pretty much. I think that we are getting some good experience there, and the faculty seem really supportive. Don't you think?" replied Andy turning to Lisa.

"I do," agreed Lisa.

Finally, Lisa and Andy exchanged looks with a slight nod toward the door.

"Mr. and Mrs. Sanders," said Andy, "we're so sorry about what happened. If we can do anything to help, please let us know."

"Thanks so much for coming to see her," said Don.

"Yes, it's so nice to know that Jodi has such good friends," added Linda.

Lisa and Andy left their phone numbers on a slip of paper and handed it to Mrs. Sanders. Saying their goodbyes, they retraced their steps to the elevator. The ride back to campus was quiet as they pondered what they had seen.

"We've got to find her notebook," said Lisa.

Chapter 5

2013, November 15,
Friday

Campus Safety Officer Steven Davis watched from a distance as a young woman with dark hair emerged quietly from the office of Professor Rathburn on the third floor of the Swensen Science Building. From his vantage point sitting on a bench down the hall, Davis had observed this event several times before, always late on a Friday afternoon, always the same dark-haired student.

In the weeks following his first such observation, Davis had contemplated how he could use this knowledge of Professor Rathburn's behavior to his advantage. He made a point of coming back and resting on this bench in the hallway of the Chemistry Department every Friday evening and was rewarded with observations of the same sequence of events. He had begun to develop ideas about what use a chemist could be to him. In his role as Campus Safety Officer, he was regularly receiving information about possible illicit drugs that he might encounter on his campus. "How easily could some of these chemists cook up a batch of one of these drugs?" he wondered. He had off-handedly let the idea drop to some of his drinking buddies and had learned a lot more about different recreational drugs and what was currently popular. And profitable. Davis and his associates had worked out a plan, and now it was time to get the ball rolling.

With a little effort, he lifted his body from the hard wooden bench and walked slowly down the terrazzo-floored hallway to Professor Rathburn's door. He tested the handle and found it locked and so knocked gently. He heard a chair squeak and the door opened. "Yes?" Professor Rathburn stood in the doorway.

"I think we should talk," stated Davis, looking around Rathburn to the interior of the office.

"Really? Why?" replied Rathburn, unmoving.

Looking him in the eye, Davis said, "Because it will be beneficial for both of us."

Feeling wary yet intrigued, Rathburn relented and stepped back to allow Davis into the room. "Ah, just who are you exactly?" Rathburn queried.

"I'm Steven Davis," he replied. "I'm in charge of all safety and security operations for the Burlington campus." He helped himself into the chair positioned beside Rathburn's desk.

"Oh, yes," said Rathburn. He vaguely recalled having seen Davis being introduced at an all-campus faculty meeting some years ago. Since the campus physical plant operations and the academic personnel had only rare encounters with each other, he wasn't surprised that he didn't remember Davis. At first glance he didn't look like anybody that he would enjoy being friends with. Davis was middle aged, overweight, and losing his hair except for a large mustache that was approaching a handlebar style. He suspected that this man drank a lot of beer and could carry on a conversation only as long as it dealt with professional football or automobile engines. "So, what can I do for you?" asked Rathburn returning to his chair.

Davis seemed to be taking his time, looking around the office and sniffing the air. "I like your perfume," he said with a little smile.

"Yes, well..." began Rathburn remembering the activities that had just recently been concluded in this room. Then, more defensively he asked, "Is that what you came here to tell me?"

Davis pulled a slip of paper out of an inside pocket of his jacket and slid it across the desk to Rathburn. "Do you know how to make this stuff?" he asked. "I'd like to get some."

Rathburn picked up the paper and read, "N-methyl-1-(3,4-methylenedioxyphenyl)-2-propanamine hydrochloride." He grabbed a sheet of paper and quickly drew a network of lines and symbols. Pausing, he studied his drawing for a moment, jotted down a few more details, paused again and then said with a note of pride, "Yes. I could make that quite easily. And I think that we have all of the necessary precursors and reagents right here in our main stockroom."

"Great," said Davis. Reaching inside his jacket once again, he produced a thick envelope and laid it on the desk in front of Rathburn. "So here is a little, ah, shall we say, 'signing bonus' for your first installment."

"Wait a minute, wait a minute," said Rathburn. "What is this stuff? And why should I, or this university even, get involved?"

"Don't you recognize it?"

"No, not immediately," he said looking back at the structures that he had drawn.

Davis smiled. "The kids call it 'Ecstasy' or 'X'. It seems to get them all jollied up and feeling good. There don't seem to be any terrible side effects. It's not like heroin or anything. And right now, a lot of money can be made if I supply this to a particular person I know, and you don't want to know. There is a lot of demand on the market for this right now."

Rathburn thought for a moment and started shaking his head. "Why in the world would I want to get mixed up in anything like this?" He pushed the paper with his drawings away.

Davis cocked his head to one side and met Rathburn's gaze. "Would it be any trouble to your reputation if your 'relationship' with a certain student were to become public?"

Rathburn shot Davis a hard look. "What are you talking about?"

"Oh come on," badgered Davis. "That young lady who just left here. The one who uses such lovely perfume." He waved his hand in the air. "I bet that she is getting pretty good grades in your class, isn't she?"

"Wait a minute. Wait a minute." Rathburn sat back barely concealing the shock that was descending on him. "How do you … You wouldn't …." he began, but then realized exactly what Davis was holding over him.

"Five thousand dollars," said Davis, tapping the envelope. "And that's just for starters." He could almost see the gears turning inside Rathburn's head. "Look, I don't really want to get you in trouble. But I just thought that we could kinda help each other out here. Ya know? You make a little X, and I bring us the rewards."

"I don't know…" said Rathburn shaking his head. His mind was racing. "Okay," he thought. "What are the risks?" Refusing could bring humiliation and disgrace. That was unthinkable! He glanced up at Davis whose smirking face was starting to look positively evil. Then he thought of Cynthia. He definitely did not want that relationship to end; he was enjoying it too much. And he definitely could not allow that to become publicly known. So then he considered the plus side. "Well, okay, what about agreeing to make this drug? Well, why not? I could get away with it. It wouldn't be that hard to produce. Any second-year student could do it. Who would know? All of my students' laboratory work is easy to keep secret under the protection of the grant contract that I have with SynZac. This could be big money! Still…"

"I, I don't know," he stammered. "I'm going to need a little more time to think about this."

"Are you sure?" asked Davis, no longer smiling. He started to reach for the envelope. "This is what you might call a 'limited time offer', if you know what I mean."

Rathburn looked again at the thick envelope. And what was in it for him he wondered. He cautiously peeked inside and saw a thick stack of $100 bills. What could he do with a little extra income? The University certainly wasn't paying him what he was worth. Perhaps this was just the opportunity that he needed to get some of the perks that he deserved.

"Okay, okay," Rathburn finally said. "But I have some requirements, too. For one, you and I will have to meet someplace else. Second, if I am going to keep this a secret, which is going to be important for both you and me," he added peering over the top of his glasses, "you are going to have to deal with the vagaries of my schedule. The synthetic steps take time, and I am going to have to arrange this so that the work gets done in such a way that nobody catches on to what is going on. That means that I'll deliver to you when a batch gets done and not before. And we are not going to be able to just whip more out at the drop of a hat. Understand?"

"Okay," agreed Davis. "How long do you think it will be until you can have the first shipment ready?"

Rathburn looked at a calendar open on his desk. "I'm going to do the first batch myself, but then I am going to have to bring in some student help. I can probably have half a kilo ready in about two weeks. We'll see how that goes and then we'll have to talk about whether there are going to be any more batches."

Davis looked doubtful.

"Look," Rathburn replied, "the students won't have a clue about what they're making. We are just going to have to wait and see how much I can actually get done here. This isn't a simple thing that you're asking. And it's got to be kept secret in the middle of all that is going on, with students and classes and… whatever." He waved his arm in the direction of the hallway.

"Okay Professor, we'll see how it goes." Davis hoisted his bulk out of the chair. "We've got a deal." He offered his hand to Rathburn who hesitated only a second and then took it. "I'll be in touch about the best way for you to contact me and we'll set up a meeting then." Davis left the room and closed the door behind him.

Rathburn sat at his desk and thumbed through the stack of bills pondering what had just transpired. "This won't be so hard. And yes, there is a lot I could do with an extra five thou coming in twice a month. Yes." He thought of Cynthia and smiled.

Chapter 6

2016, April 6,
Wednesday evening

Back on campus, Lisa and Andy had returned to the library. The need to study for their courses could not be ignored for long. The lengthening days of April in Superior, Wisconsin seemed to provide some hope for cheerier times ahead, but still the grey skies and cold winds could descend upon the barely budded trees of the campus to remind all that winter had not yet totally relinquished its grip. Hunched against the growing cold, Andy and Lisa left the library for a second time that day to trek to the SC for the last dinner serving.

Most of the evening crowd of students had departed from the brightly lit cafeteria where Lisa and Andy sat and finished their meal. Andy was pretty tolerant of the cafeteria cuisine, but Lisa was tired of it and usually preferred to fix her own meals in her apartment off campus. They both had partial food contracts that allowed them to eat some of their meals on campus when it was convenient. At other times they prepared their own food or patronized commercial restaurants in town.

Lisa was still mulling over her frustration at not remembering what Jodi had been working on. "I'm going to go back to the lab to see whether I can find Jodi's notebook," she told Andy.

"Do you think that you'll be able to get in? The labs are usually locked when there are no profs in the building. I doubt that any of them are still around at this time."

"Mariah has a key in her desk," stated Lisa. "She's allowed to have a master key to all the lab rooms because her assistantship is for prepping for the teaching labs."

"Alright," said Andy.

"I know where she keeps it. Come on."

The two hiked across the campus as the last glow of the sunset faded in the west. They climbed the steps to the third-floor lounge where chemistry students often remained in the building between their classes. Chemistry majors, students working on research projects for different professors and students assigned to assisting in a teaching laboratory could request to have access to a private desk in this room. The lounge provided a secure place to leave their belongings and encouraged a feeling of camaraderie between the students who hung out there. Whiteboards and a large periodic table on the walls facilitated the pursuit of discussions outside of class, while a couple of overstuffed chairs, a refrigerator, microwave and coffee pot contributed to the coziness. It was a pleasant place for students to congregate between classes and fostered a sense of belonging in the department.

Inside the room Andy and Lisa found several of their classmates, Mariah Jackson, Kayla Martin, Jamie Perrin and Gary Pollan engaged in discussion. Books and notebooks were open on their desks, but they had rotated their chairs toward each other. "Any alkoxy group would be an ortho-para director," dark-haired Mariah was saying, "it doesn't have to be specifically methoxy." The three looked up and stopped their discussion as Lisa and Andy came in.

"Mariah, could we borrow your lab key?" asked Lisa. "There is something in the research lab that I want to look at."

"I guess…," said Mariah. "But be sure to lock up afterwards and bring it back." She extracted a key from the back of her top desk drawer and handed it to Lisa.

The door to the research lab complex was a short way down the hall. Lisa unlocked the door and went in with Andy close behind. Immediately they could smell the chemicals that were sprayed into the room by Jodi's explosion. "Smells like vinegar," muttered Andy, sniffing.

"You mean acetic acid," corrected Lisa. "I bet that was the solvent she was using."

Approaching Jodi's work area, they could see that much of the mess had been left as it was immediately after the explosion. Wide "DO NOT CROSS" yellow tape had been strung around the scene at several levels. A dark stain on the floor marked the spot where Jodi's blood had pooled when she had fallen. Lisa circled the area scanning over the debris. "Do you see her lab notebook in there?" she asked Andy. I know that she had it. She was holding it in her hands when I first came in. It should be right there, on the floor, or on the bench." The two studied the area. The sink basin was empty. The shelves down the center of the benches contained only reagent bottles, and the benches across from and adjacent to the fume hood were mostly bare. A few round flasks with yellow plastic caps containing unknown mixtures sat on cork rings waiting for further processing. Andy approached Jodi's hood area from the far side and ducked under the yellow tape.

"What are you doing?" Lisa hissed. "You're not supposed to be in there."

"Just looking," answered Andy. Tiptoeing around a few pieces of glass, he systematically started opening and shutting the drawers below the bench counters. One after one, nothing was revealed except collections of glassware and various tools. "It's just not here anywhere," he said.

"Damn!" Lisa breathed. "Where can it be?" The two of them continued to scan the benches and the surrounding area, looking in cupboards and drawers, but the notebook was nowhere to be found.

"Well, I guess that's it," said Lisa, "Let's go."

"Wait a sec," said Andy, "I've got an idea." Speaking in a hushed tone Andy began, "Look. We can figure out what she was working on. Most of it is still here." He indicated the jumbled mass of glass and metal strewn across the floor of her hood. A wastebasket standing in the aisle was still stuffed with paper towels that had been used to mop up the floor.

"Good idea," said Lisa, brightening. "I'll get something to put these in," she said indicating the chemical-soaked towels. Lisa went to her work area and came back with a plastic bucket and a pair of tongs. Reaching between the yellow tapes she grabbed the wastebasket and pulled it closer. She used the tongs to pick out the sodden paper towels, stuffed them into her bucket, and took them back to her work area.

Andy, who had gone out of the room for a few minutes, returned carrying a small vial. "It's a SPME fiber," he explained, "Solid Phase Micro Extraction. It'll absorb the odors, and we'll be able to run it through the mass spec." Lisa nodded in appreciation. Andy opened the vial and pulled out a thin black fiber attached to the cap. Reaching through the yellow tape, he placed the vial and upside-down cap in amongst the debris just inside Jodi's hood. Just as he had set it down, they heard footsteps of someone coming into the room.

"What are you doing there?" a voice demanded. Turning, Lisa recognized Mr. Davis, the campus Safety Officer.

"Ah, we were just looking," replied Andy.

"Well, this area is off limits," stated Davis. "All of this," he waved his hand in the direction of the taped off area and hood, "must remain untouched until after the state safety inspectors and the insurance people have been here. So don't touch anything." He stood there looking directly at the two of them.

"Ah, Mr. Davis," Lisa ventured, "were you the person that put up this yellow tape?"

"Yeah. Why do you want to know?"

"I was wondering, did you happen to see Jodi's lab notebook?"

Davis studied her for a moment, and then said, "What business is it of yours?"

Lisa quickly debated whether she should take Davis into her confidence. Davis' brusque demeanor dissuaded her from continuing. "None, I guess," she said glumly. "Come on, Andy, let's go."

Andy looked briefly at the SPME fiber that was left standing in the hood. For anybody who didn't know it was there it would be completely lost to view in the jumble. "Okay, I'm coming."

The two exited the research lab with Davis following. Stepping out into the corridor, Davis locked the door and waited while Andy and Lisa walked down the hall back to the student assistants' lounge.

"Later," said Andy in a hushed voice.

Feeling chastened, they went back to the student assistants' room, returned Mariah's key, and chatted a while with the other students. Mariah, Kayla, Jamie and Gary all wanted to hear more from Lisa about the explosion. Finally Lisa asked the others, "Did you see the EMTs take Jodi out of the building?" All four of them had. "Was her notebook with her or did you see anybody take it?"

"I don't think so," stated Jamie. "I was in the room when they came in. They just picked her up and put her on that stretcher thing. Then they covered her with a blanket. That was it. I didn't see any notebook."

Lisa pondered for a moment. "Well, thanks. I guess we'll just have to wait for it to turn up."

"Rathburn was there, though," Gary added. "He seemed to be paying attention to Lisa's things, like her goggles and stuff. He was poking around on her benchtop."

Andy and Lisa looked at each other as they took this in. Finally the topic of the explosion was exhausted and the discussion of electrophilic aromatic substitution resumed. Andy and Lisa headed for the exit, but when they got to the steps outside Lisa stopped. "Something's fishy," she said. "Jodi had her notebook in her hand when I came into the room, the explosion happened, and now… no notebook."

"Yeah," Andy agreed. They pondered this as they looked out across the darkened campus and sniffed the cool night air. "But we'll be able to figure out what she was working with," said Andy. "I can run that SPME fiber through the mass spec, and you can try to figure out what chemicals are soaked in those towels. We can do this, don't you think?"

Lisa thought a moment and then said, "Are you going back to the library?"

"Yeah. I guess so," replied Andy. "You?"

"Nah. I'm going to finish up at home. Okay? See you tomorrow."

Wistfully Andy watched Lisa depart. Then he turned and headed back to the library.

Chapter 7

2013, November 18, Monday

Charles Rathburn's ten o'clock organic chemistry class had come to its conclusion for the day. Although large chalkboards completely covered the front of the small auditorium, they were no longer used. Instead, professors used tablet computers, on which one could draw with a stylus, connected to the room's overhead digital projector to make their writing and images appear on a large screen. The computer connections made it easier for instructors to supplement their PowerPoint presentations with video clips or digressions to an internet site or other source. Gone were the days of clapping erasers and chalk dust. Students were stuffing their notebooks into their backpacks. Those planning to exit the building were donning their coats against the chill northern Wisconsin November weather. Others slung their coats over their arms as they progressed to another class in the same building or simply planned to delay their departure for a while.

"Miss Collins," Professor Rathburn called as he spied Cynthia descending the risers by his lectern. Now that Charles and Cynthia had established a pattern of meeting in his office on Friday afternoons, discretion had motivated them to agree that they would keep their contact to a minimum at other times.

"Yes, Professor?" said Cynthia, not resisting the temptation to allow a coy smile to show.

For the benefit of any casual onlookers, Rathburn managed to keep a stern visage. Looking over the top of his glasses he said, "We need to talk. Please come to my office." He led the way through the hall of milling students without encouraging her to walk with him. In his office he partially closed his door to the hubbub outside and became more friendly. Imparting one of his rare smiles he asked, "How have you been?"

"I'm doing fine," she replied noncommittally, somewhat puzzled as to what this was going to be about.

Leaning back in his chair, Rathburn hesitated and played with a pen on his desk. Finally he said, "I have a proposal to make. It has several parts, so please hear me out."

Fully attentive now, Cynthia settled more firmly into her chair. "Okay."

"First," he began, "I need somebody to do some lab work for me. You are a chem major, so you could use the research credit. I know that you are only halfway through your sophomore coursework, but the skills required for the work that I need done are mostly ones you have already been exposed to, and I will assist you in anything that would be new." He looked up to see whether she was showing signs of agreement or not. "Second," he went on, watching her more closely now, "I am wondering whether you would accept an offer from me? I have rented an apartment that overlooks Old Central Park here in Superior. It's quite nice and has a great view of the lake. You could live there. It would be yours, but I would pay the rent. And I would have a key, too." He paused to see whether she understood the meaning in this last remark. Assured that she was both aware and interested, he added, "It would be a much nicer place for you and me to meet. What do you think?"

It didn't take Cynthia long to grasp what an attractive offer was being presented. Working in Rathburn's research group would be somewhat of an honor. It implied that when she graduated and moved on that she would be accorded a favorable letter of recommendation. Very likely this would open doors for her getting into a job or graduate school. And it would allow her to develop and practice her skills as a chemist. The second part of the offer was also eminently attractive. She would love to get out of the run-down place that she currently lived in with Peter and four other roommates. Having her own private space in a posh neighborhood in Superior sounded like a dream come true. And having a bed in which to entertain Dr. Rathburn held all sorts of exciting imaginings for her.

"Why, yes, Charles, I think that both of those ideas are great," she said trying not to sound too eager.

Rathburn's first instinct was to bristle at Cynthia's use of the familiar

'Charles', but he realized that in consideration of the intimacy of their relationship it would have to be regarded as appropriate. In fact, he realized that such a level of intimacy and familiarity was exactly what he was hoping to arrange with Cynthia by setting her up in the Old Central Park apartment.

"I'm so pleased to hear that you will accept, Cynthia," said Rathburn, leaning forward and briefly touching the back of her hand. Remembering his partially open office door and his desire not to make any displays while other students and faculty were in the building, he quickly withdrew.

"I will arrange for lab space for you in the student research lab, clear out some drawers, and get a fume hood ready. We can get you started in there by the end of this week. Oh, and you can have a private desk in the student assistants' lounge, too. I'll find out which one and let you know." He jotted some notes on a pad. "As for the second item," he turned to look at her, "the lease starts on January first. I can arrange for a couple of men with a truck to help you move your belongings if need be. Do you have much?"

"No," replied Cynthia. "What I have will fit in two suitcases and a couple of boxes. It will all fit in my car in one load," she added somewhat forlornly.

"No problem," said Rathburn. "The apartment will be furnished. There are some housewares for cooking and so on. When you, ah, we get in there you can decide whether there are any amenities that you would like to add. Okay?"

They considered each other in silence for a moment, both imagining what this new arrangement was going to mean for each of them. Cynthia spoke first. "Thank you, Charles. You are very kind."

Charles nodded and smiled at her. Cynthia rose and started to collect her things preparing to leave.

"Oh, one more thing, Cynthia."

"Yes?" She sat back down.

"Just out of curiosity," he began, "have you ever tried the drug, Ecstasy?"

Cynthia paused wondering whether a right or wrong answer could have consequences regarding the arrangement that they had just agreed upon. Deciding that the truth wasn't going to hurt she said, "Yeah. A few times."

"What's it like?" asked Rathburn.

She sensed that his inquiry was due to genuine interest and was not judgmental. "Well, it's actually very nice," she began. "It makes you feel energized. Um, it makes you feel, well, like you are connected to the other people around you, in a way. You kinda feel your skin. You're aware of touching. It's nice. But the next day can feel kinda slow, though. It's okay, I guess." She looked up to see how he was taking this.

Rathburn nodded. "Just wondering."

Sensing that their conversation was ended, Cynthia rose and stepped out into the hall. "Hmmm, I wonder what that was about?"

Chapter 8

**2013, December 10,
Tuesday**

A low brick building near the corner of Banks Ave. and 5th St. in the warehouse district of Superior provided a suitable home for the Sea Shanty Saloon. It was nestled between two aging brick commercial buildings and sat across the street from a large warehouse and yards where all manner of goods were transferred from shipping vessels to railroad cars and vice versa. Stacks of pallets, shipping containers, boxes, sacks and bins of all sizes came and went, day after day, as the commerce of the region streamed through the twin ports of Superior, Wisconsin and Duluth, Minnesota. With this movement of goods there was also the movement of men and women, workers who labored at the various tasks demanded by this activity. Some stayed for only a short while, moving on to other jobs or another region of the country. Some stayed longer, getting to know the system, and rising in responsibility for overseeing the operations. But they rarely rose very far above a minimal level of payment for their work, or very far above a basic level in their social standing.

The Shanty had little to advertise it, just one neon beer sign in a high window. The interior was dimly lit and once was decorated with ropes and fishing nets, a kind of nautical theme that was now largely ignored. Just inside the door a tall glass-fronted cooler boasted a limited assortment of six-packs of off-sale beer. Next to the cooler was a long bar with several small colorfully lighted signs on the wall illuminating the various bottles stacked below. Along the opposite knotty-pine paneled wall was a series of small tables with chairs for the few patrons that perhaps came with a partner and preferred seating other than a bar stool. At the back of the room there was just enough space for a pool table that was kept busy by the stream of men who came through. Beyond that was a hallway with doors labeled His and Hers. A turn in the hallway at the back of the building led to a stairway down to a basement that presumably housed the stock of liquor and beer, and in the other direction, a steel door opened onto a gravel and cigarette butt-covered parking area that had more than once been the site of an unfair and brutal fight.

Shortly after ten p.m. Steven Davis pushed in through the front door carrying a dark colored cloth satchel. After a cursory stamping of his feet to shake off the light snow that had been falling, he selected a seat at one of the small tables and unobtrusively placed the satchel under the table against the wall. With a bit more show he shrugged his coat onto the back of the chair and stepped across the aisle to the bar. The bartender was a large man who clearly would be as adept as a bouncer as he would likely be at serving drinks. He seemed to recognize Davis and correctly anticipated his drink order by reaching for a cold tall beer glass. "What'll it be?" he asked.

"Ya got Leinies on tap?" replied Davis.

"Sure thing," was the reply as he pulled the handle.

Davis returned to his seat sipping the foam from the top of his glass. Glancing around the room he took in the view of the other patrons. Three younger men sporting multiple tattoos and piercings were playing pool while two older men were huddled beside each other in conversation at the bar. As Davis sat and sipped his beer, two figures rose from their seats at the back of the room and sauntered up to Davis' table carrying their partially consumed beers. "Hello, Steve," said one.

"Hello Caleb, hello Dugan," replied Davis.

Caleb Murrow and Dugan Jones appeared to be cast from the same mold. Both were in their mid-to-late fifties, under six feet tall, balding, and losing their muscular builds to middle-age paunches. Similarly, both seemed to feel that the best way to deal with the world was to present a gruff, unfriendly exterior. "Hey. Have a seat," said Davis and motioned to his table. Caleb and Dugan sat on one side with Davis on the other and they all regarded each other.

"Come on. Relax," offered Davis, taking a swig from his glass. The others followed suit as if on command.

Finally Dugan asked, "Well, ya got something for me?"

"Yeah, but what's your hurry?" said Davis. "C'mon. Take it easy. Enjoy the ambiance." He waved his hand in the direction of the bar. Caleb and Dugan shifted their gaze to the bartender and then looked at each other and shrugged.

"Okay," said Dugan. He took a sip of beer.

After a minute of silence, Davis nodded his head slightly in the direction of the satchel under the table. "It's here. And it should be pretty high quality. Have your guys check it out."

Dugan nodded without any show of emotion. "I'm sure they will."

Davis continued, "I should be able to keep this coming pretty regularly. I'll be contacting you when the next package is ready."

Dugan nodded and a look of satisfaction crossed his face. "Sounds good, Steve. This will go over well upstairs."

"Yeah, well it should."

The three sipped their beers in silence and looked around the room. The bartender sat on a stool by the cash register near the front of the room reading a paperback novel while an occasional "click" of colliding pool balls could be heard from the back. After a short while Davis drained the end of his beer and stood. "Okay, I'll be in touch," he said hoisting his heavy coat to his shoulders.

"The check is in the mail," said Dugan with mock cheerfulness.

"Yeah, right."

Leaving the satchel under the table, Davis exchanged waves with the bartender, pushed the door open and stepped into the cold. He paused a moment on the sidewalk and scanned the street up and down, checking to see whether anyone might be watching, though he didn't expect anybody would be. His car was parked beside the warehouse across the street, and it never hurt to be cautious. When he had settled into his car, he checked the time on his cell phone. Five minutes later he saw two heavy-set figures with a cloth satchel emerge from the Shanty, turn, and walk up the street. Abruptly they turned and stepped into the street walking directly toward the parking lot where he was sitting. Davis slouched down as far as the steering wheel would allow and pulled his hat down to shade his face. Out the side window he could see the two men cut diagonally across the parking lot and head to a side door of the warehouse. They paused under the lamp that hung above the door and then went inside. "Good boys," he thought, "straight home to mama." Checking his watch again, he waited for fifteen minutes. When nothing more happened, he straightened up, started the engine, and headed home.

Chapter 9

2016, April 7,
Thursday morning

Thursday morning the campus was once again the site of throngs of students walking casually, yet purposefully from building to building. Spring-like weather had returned, at least for the time being. The sunshine was warm and brought students to the outdoors like new seedlings sprouting after a spring rain. Those who didn't have a scheduled class, and some who did, were carrying coffees or sodas and congregating on the lawns and benches that bedecked the campus mall. Andy, Gary, Mariah, and Kayla were gathered at a picnic table delaying their inevitable return to their classes. Lisa, wearing jeans and a navy-blue Burlington U sweatshirt, was approaching from the direction of the SC carrying her books and a large insulated mug.

She stopped by their table and announced, "I'm going to talk to Rathburn."

Andy got up from where he had been sitting. "I'm coming with you."

"Good luck with that," muttered Gary as he watched them go. Gary Pollan still harbored a degree of animosity for Rathburn since the day over a year ago when Rathburn had embarrassed him severely in front of his entire class. The weekend prior to this humiliating event had been busy for Gary. While he had planned to spend it studying for his Monday morning organic exam, a burst pipe in the basement of the rental house where he had an upstairs room intervened.

Fortunately for Gary, the burst pipe and resulting flood did not affect any of his possessions. But the housemate who occupied the basement apartment had not fared so well. Gary pitched in to help, first getting the water turned off, calling the landlord, and then trying to rescue his friend's belongings. The friend knew of another off-campus apartment that had a spare room, and he was able to move his belongings across town to this new location. Gary volunteered his jeep and spent the afternoon making trips to the new apartment. Meanwhile, the water was shut off for all of Gary's house until the following Monday, which meant that he was without his usual cooking, showering and toilet facilities. Gary's performance on the exam Monday morning had not been his best, and on Wednesday, when Rathburn was returning the graded papers, he made a point of publicly belittling Gary's work. Although student grades are supposed to be a private matter, from time-to-time Rathburn would pick out one student for ridicule. Perhaps the neatly dressed professor from the East Coast was offended by Gary's rumpled army surplus style of dress. Or perhaps it was because Gary's physical size intimidated him. For whatever reason, Rathburn announced that Gary's score on the exam was the lowest in the class. Even then, Rathburn didn't let it drop. He continued for at least another two minutes berating Gary, implying that his performance showed that he was both lazy and inept, and that he was probably not "college material". Gary was never given an opportunity to offer an explanation or defense.

  More than one student had less than warm feelings for the Professor. Charles Rathburn appeared to have a very high opinion of himself and an equally low opinion of everybody else. In his interactions with students, he tended to be authoritative, squelching any comments that hinted toward criticism or disagreement with whatever he said. He wore expensive-looking clothes and drove a red Mazda MX-5 Miata that he seemed to think would make him irresistible to all the female students. He was often difficult to find on campus, regularly ignoring his own posted office hours. Carrying on a conversation with him usually involved letting oneself in for some form of criticism or revelation of one's own failings which were happily pointed out by Professor Rathburn and brought front and center as the reason for one's own troubles. Four years earlier, Rathburn had somehow won a $500,000 five-year research grant from SynZac Corporation. This had given him a certain amount of fame on campus, but really had worsened his interactions with his colleagues and students. Although he now had funds with which he could support research students generously, he still had trouble attracting students to work with him. Jodi Sanders had accepted his offer largely because of her more needful financial situation. It was also known that Cynthia Collins worked for Rathburn, though that appointment was a source of some puzzlement among the senior chemistry students. It did not go unnoticed that Rathburn tended to invite mainly good-looking female students into his research group.

Lisa and Andy climbed the stairs to the third floor and walked in the direction of Dr. Rathburn's office. "Mid-morning on a Thursday, one should be able to find a professor," she muttered. But his door was closed, and there was no response to her knocking.

"Tell you what, if you want to wait here, I'm going to go retrieve that SPME fiber," said Andy.

"Okay," she replied. "I guess I'll hang here for a little while. If he doesn't turn up soon, I'll see you in the lounge."

Andy set off down the hall while Lisa leaned against the wall across from Rathburn's door. Within a few minutes she had grown impatient and decided to leave. Just then, she saw Rathburn approaching. "Dr. Rathburn, may I speak with you?" she began.

"So. Have you seen the light? You want to join my group?" he asked unsmilingly as he worked his key in the lock. "Had enough of old Gerry Barton?"

"No, sir. That is not the reason," she replied, trying to sound respectful.

"Well, what is it?" he said coldly, opening the door. Rathburn proceeded into his office and sat without offering a seat to Lisa. Turning to his computer, he woke it up, occasionally typing and mousing as he grudgingly gave Lisa his divided attention.

After what she thought was a respectful pause, Lisa asked, "Do you know how Jodi is doing?"

Rathburn stopped his mousing and looked at her as if to say it was none of her business, but replied, "I hear that she is still unconscious, but is likely to recover." He gave no indication that he was at all concerned for her well-being.

Lisa tried again. "I was wondering whether you could tell me what she was working on last Tuesday? You see, she asked me to check something in her notebook just before the explosion happened, but I never got to see what it was. I thought that if I could see it, we could figure out what went wrong." She used the "we" hoping to enlist his cooperation. "Do you know where her notebook is?" she asked.

"No. I have no idea where it is," he said quickly. His gaze wavered and he briefly glanced to the table beside his desk. Lisa followed his gaze to a stack of student notebooks on the table. Rathburn cleared his throat and she turned back to look at him.

Professor Rathburn seemed to gather himself in his chair and then he leaned forward and stared hard at Lisa. "First of all, young lady, the work that we do for SynZac is proprietary. That means that information relating to my work for them is to be kept secure and not to be revealed to the public in any way, shape, manner or form. So that means that you should just leave the investigating up to the authorities and go back to your studies. Got it?"

Lisa sat, unspeaking, looking at Rathburn's unfriendly visage. She pondered whether to reveal that she and Andy had spent some time looking, albeit unsuccessfully, for Jodi's notebook in the research lab, but decided that rather than be considered helpful, she would probably just garner another reprimand.

Rathburn stood and indicated that Lisa should depart. She rose and stepped out of the office. Turning back, she said softly, "I'm sorry that Jodi got hurt. I hope that she will be okay."

"I do, too," said Rathburn flatly as he shut the door behind her.

With her books held close to her chest, Lisa walked slowly to the student assistants' lounge at the far end of the corridor. "Well, that was wholly unproductive," she thought. "Who am I to think that I might be able to help?" She dropped her books on her desk and sat staring at the large periodic table on the wall. "Now what?" she wondered.

Minutes later Mariah, Gary, and Kayla trooped into the room. "So how did that go?" Kayla asked.

Lisa scowled and made a farting noise. "Pfft. He told me that it was secret information and that nobody knows where her notebook is. And that I should be a good girl and mind my own business," she added. "Why is it that he seems like such a liar? He told me flat out that he has no idea where her notebook is."

Without looking up from his desk, Jamie, who had been listening, chimed in, "That's what we in the analytical business call a 'false negative'." Kayla smirked.

Returning to seriousness, Lisa asked, "I wonder if he cares about Jodi at all?"

"I doubt it," said Kayla glumly.

"I'm not surprised," chimed in Gary. "The man is a scoundrel."

"Scoundrel?" echoed Kayla mockingly. "That's a pretty serious accusation there, buster," she added with a smile.

"I'm just tempering my language for polite company," said Gary, winking back at her.

"Does anybody know what it is he is supposed to be doing for SynZac?"

asked Lisa. "Jodi was working on something that must have been related to that. That's why Rathburn claims that it is proprietary, so he doesn't have to tell anybody what she was doing."

"Perhaps you should talk to Cynthia," suggested Mariah, "She's working for him, too."

The suggestion elicited general agreement, but nobody moved to do anything about it. Sensing an end to the topic, they turned to their own desks and busied themselves with other matters.

Chapter 10

The padded room that once served as the workout area for the University's wrestling team was located in the basement of the Heikkinen Athletic Complex on the east side of the Burlington campus. Protective mats covered every inch of the floor, lined the walls to a height of about six feet and surrounded the two posts in the middle of the room. In the 1990s, interest in wrestling as a sport had waned and eventually the program was cancelled by the administration. For several years the room lay idle, but then an interest developed in co-ed classes in martial arts and self-defense. The University could not afford to hire a faculty person with such a specialty, so the classes were offered sporadically when a suitable instructor could be hired on a limited part-time basis. Recently a martial arts club had been formed, and so the old wrestling room had become the club's dojo. Student fees helped to pay for a club advisor who could be an instructor and supervise organized activities with a modicum of university oversight.

Gary Pollan stood at the front of the room, finishing up the karate regimen. Although he was currently taking classes with many of the students before him, Gary was older, having spent several years in the Army after high school and before coming to Burlington. Because of his martial arts expertise, the university had hired him to serve as the club's advisor and organize and lead two classes, one specifically in karate and a second in basic self-defense tactics. Fifteen students, barefoot and dressed in white gis, were arrayed in three rows in front of the instructors. Gary, at one hundred and eighty-five pounds and standing a little over six feet tall, wore a black belt at his waist and made a commanding presence. He was flanked by two assistant instructors who were two of the more advanced students. One had earned a brown belt before coming to Burlington. The other was still a white belt, although somewhat more experienced than the others in the class. One of the assistants was counting out loud as the class executed a series of punches in mid-air. ".... thirty-eight, thirty-nine, forty, forty-one…"

"Fifty of these, and then two sets of katas. That'll be enough for today," thought Gary. He walked through the rows, lifting arms here, straightening shoulders there, correcting lapses in form in a gentle yet commanding fashion. This wasn't like the karate dojos that he had belonged to overseas in the military or briefly in California when he had returned to civilian life. There, any fault would have merited a punishment, extra push-ups on one's knuckles, or extra punches. Here the participants were all voluntary. If he was too severe, the students would quit, enrollment would drop, and he would be out of a paid gig that he enjoyed. He didn't especially care for harsh discipline, and he could see no reason to be overly demanding. The participants wanted to learn, and generally the desired outcome of having their skill level improve was more effectively accomplished by kind encouragement and correction, rather than degrading punishment. "Except…" he thought as the door thumped opened and a student stepped into the room. "Peter Dahle. Late again," he thought. "Why does he even bother? We're almost done for today." Gary pointed to a place in the back. Peter bowed faintly to the room, sauntered to his position and joined in executing punches in the air.

A short while later the class in the traditional kneeling position bowed to the instructors and then broke for the locker rooms, talking quietly. Two of the student participants who Gary knew well, Andy and Kayla, approached him as the others filtered out the door. "Sensei…" Andy began, and then, "May I call you Gary now that class is over?"

"Sure," replied Gary with a smile. "What is it?"

"We're going to get a group together tonight to look at that worksheet that Martinelli gave us yesterday. Do you want to join us?"

"That would be great," agreed Gary. "But I've arranged to meet some friends later, so I can't stay much beyond about 8:30. Okay?"

"I'm sure that'll be fine. We're going to start around 7:00 in the student assistants' room. See you then." They turned and headed for the door. Kayla lingered just long enough to catch Gary's eye and give him a little smile and wave. "Meet you in the hall, after?" she asked pointing toward the door.

Acknowledging their earlier agreement to go to the cafeteria together after their workout, Gary nodded.

Gary looked around the room, hoping to catch Peter Dahle before he left. "That guy needs to know that his late arrivals are just not acceptable," he thought. Stepping into the hallway he immediately encountered Peter leaning over and talking to a short blonde female student. Peter's smile disappeared when he saw Gary. "Peter, could we talk?" Gary asked.

The young woman excused herself but not before flashing Peter a quick wink. "See you later," she said with a meaningful smile.

Peter slouched against the wall. "Yeah?"

Gary considered the sassy defensiveness in Peter's body language and the tone of his reply. Quelling an initial feeling of anger, he spoke quietly and as politely as he could. "I find it disruptive when you arrive late, Peter. A serious martial arts club expects a level of discipline where its members arrive on time. Please be on time in the future. And if you're late, then please don't come in at all. Okay?"

"Yeah?" said Peter. "You're not in charge here. You're a student just like I am. I don't have to do what you say. I paid my fees, so I have every right to be here whenever I want to."

Gary thought briefly how easy it would be to lay Peter out flat in three seconds, but then sighed. It just seemed sad that Peter couldn't grasp what was important in this situation. Gary looked Peter in the eye for a moment and said quietly. "But I am in charge here, Peter. I'm paid by the University to be the advisor to this club and the instructor for this class. And I'm telling you that your late arrivals are inappropriate. Don't let it happen again." Without waiting for a reply Gary stepped around Peter and headed for the locker room.

"Yeah, whatever," muttered Peter when Gary was beyond earshot.

After showering and changing, Gary climbed the stairs to the main lobby where he found the area empty of students. He dropped his gym bag on a bench and walked to the windows, attempting to peer out into the darkness that had settled on the campus outside. He knew that he would weather the issue with Peter, but the conflict still left him feeling unsettled. The sound of approaching footsteps changed his thoughts to a happier topic, namely Kayla. Kayla, with her athletic body, long reddish-brown hair, friendly smile, and a totally charming smattering of freckles across her nose and cheeks was always a welcome presence in Gary's day. The previous fall they had by chance taken seats next to each other in one of their classes, and since then they had continued to keep company, eventually proceeding to a more exclusive association that their friends would classify as 'dating'. Gary was comforted by Kayla's easy-going disposition. Nothing much seemed to upset her. She was happy to be in college and was satisfied with average grades. Although unsure about any long-term career plans, she went through her day with a confidence that everything was going to work out for the best. Gary found her to be an uplifting and calming influence that he was pleased to have in his life.

"Hey there, big guy," she greeted him coming up the stairs. Kayla was wearing a sky-blue pullover sweater, dark skinny jeans, and black ankle boots. "Wanna grab some din-din?"

"I'd like to grab you," he replied giving her an enthusiastic hug.

"Woo hoo!" she smiled. "There'll be time for that later. But let's go. I'm hungry."

They donned their winter coats, grabbed their gym bags and pushed out the door. Proceeding west to the SC, Kayla linked her arm through Gary's, walking close to him.

"That Peter is such a jerk," began Gary.

After a short silence, Kayla replied, "Don't let him get to you. Remember, he's temporary."

"Temporary?"

"Yeah. We'll all be graduating in six weeks. Right? Two months from now we'll all have gone our separate ways. You'll never see him again. He's not worth getting worked up about now."

"Yeah, temporary," agreed Gary. "That's a good way to think of him."

The cafeteria in the SC still seemed bleak in spite of all the bright lighting and colored walls. At this time of day, at this time of the year the large glass windows all looked black, which gave an unassailable overcast to the room. Gary and Kayla dropped their belongings by the entrance and visited the different stations, finally settling into plastic chairs by a table for two. After an initial eating frenzy, their pace slackened, and conversation became possible. Kayla started by telling of news from her home in Hayward, Wisconsin. Her parents owned and operated a corner restaurant that specialized in nothing, but nevertheless featured great standard American fare. Until she had left for college, Kayla, her parents and three younger siblings all shared the apartment that occupied the space above the restaurant. Homelife had been good. Her parents were loving and attentive, insistent upon good behavior, and supportive of each child's interests. Kayla chattered away about what her siblings were doing in school and sports and how the weather was affecting the family business. The influx of cross-country skiers and snowmobilers was pretty much over for the winter, and the fishermen had not yet arrived.

Gary liked listening to Kayla talk about her home life. It sounded so normal and wholesome. He wished that he could be a part of it. His background had been quite different. While Gary was growing up as an only child in Two Harbors, Minnesota, Gary's father had worked long hours in the taconite plant there and carried on a sideline as a fixit-man and locksmith. His mother had been a closet drinker and pretty much left Gary to fend for himself through school and afterwards. She had left the home when Gary was beginning high school, and Gary lived with his dad, hung out with friends, trying to stay out of trouble, and barely outrunning the long arm of the law on several occasions. Fortunately, the wild north woods could absorb most of his hijinks, and he never got into any real scrapes with the law. The friends that he planned to meet that night were two of his high school buddies, Chuck Murphy and Randy Karr. Gary and Randy had both signed up for the army right out of high school, but Chuck had stayed in Duluth working in an automobile garage. Since Randy and Gary had gotten out of the service, the three of them liked to get together periodically, drink beer, shoot some pool, and reminisce about their past escapades.

Finally Gary turned to a topic that had been on his mind. "Have you thought about what you are going to do next year?" he asked.

Kayla idly examined the tips of several strands of her hair as she contemplated the question. "I'm not sure."

"There's a job fair down in Minneapolis next weekend. Do you want to go?"

Kayla considered this and then said, "My parents would like me to move back to Hayward. They think that I will be able to help with the restaurant and my brothers."

"But that would hardly use your degree, at all, though," countered Gary.

"I know, but, if I go to the job fair, most of the jobs are going to be far away from Hayward."

"Maybe you could find something in Duluth. That wouldn't be too far."

"I know…"

"And besides, Kayla, someday you're just going to have to get out on your own. Don't you think?"

"Yeah," she nodded glumly. "So what are you going to do next year?"

"Well, I've applied to three graduate schools: UMD, NDSU and UND, but I haven't heard anything final from any of them. If I don't get into one of those,

I guess I'll be looking for a job, too."

"So, you don't really know where you are going either. You could be going anywhere."

"True," said Gary. He reached beside their trays and picked up Kayla's hand. "I was kinda hoping that somehow we might find a way to… you know." He looked up into her eyes.

Kayla held his gaze for a moment, grasping his meaning. Turning to look at her phone, she said, "Hey. Time to go." They bussed their trays, collected their belongings and headed for the Science Building. Climbing the stairs to the third floor, Kayla groused, "Why does the Chemistry Department always have to be on the top floor?"

"Because it makes it easier to ventilate," replied Gary. "They think we stink."

"I 'spose we do, don't we?" Kayla chuckled.

The study session had already started when they arrived. Andy, Lisa, Mariah, and Cynthia were sitting at their desks with their chairs swiveled to face the center of the room. A few other students who did not have designated desks were interspersed. Mariah, the acknowledged leader and top student, was leading the discussion dealing with the symmetry characteristics of molecular orbitals and allowed pericyclic reactions.

An hour and a half later students were picking up their books and heading out the door, either satisfied that they had made sufficient progress or just too mentally exhausted to continue. Gary touched Kayla on the hand, "See you tomorrow, okay? I'm gonna go meet up with Chuck and Randy."

"Okay. See ya," Kayla replied. She had met Chuck and Randy on previous occasions. She knew that they and Gary were friends and basically supported each other, but they tended to be a little crude for her tastes. And when they were drinking, she was happy to be someplace else entirely. "Be good," she called after him in a motherly way. Gary laughed.

Twenty-five minutes later Gary was parking his jeep in the un-lit lot across the street from the Sea Shanty Saloon. This had been the preferred bar that Gary and his friends had frequented during their high school days. It had been an easy drive across the border from Minnesota into Wisconsin where the proprietor of the Sea Shanty was not particular about checking IDs. The payoff was that now the three of them were loyal customers. Randy and Chuck were already in the middle of a pool game when Gary came through the front door.

"Yo! Gary," they greeted him. High fives and shoulder slaps completed the ritual. Gary retrieved a bottle of beer from the bartender and grabbed a cue from the rack on the wall. "How's it going?" he asked.

"This slouch has lost his touch," chided Chuck. "I'm up three games."

"Don't worry. It won't last," retorted Randy. "I'm just setting you up for the kill."

"Right," laughed Chuck.

The evening waxed on as the games were played and the beers were consumed. After a few hours all three were playing more poorly than they had been at the start, but they were enjoying it just as much, if not more. Gary was leaning against the back wall balancing his cue on his toe when his gazed focused on a trio of men seated at a small table closer to the front of the bar. The one facing him, older, balding, heavy-set with a wannabee handle-bar mustache looked familiar. "Oh, these guys," thought Gary. He turned back to Randy and Chuck. "Hey guys," he said quietly. "See those three sitting over there by the wall?" He nodded in their direction. "Watch them a minute." They paused their game and sipped their beers while casually watching the front of the room. Soon they saw one man reach down under the table and slide a package along the wall until it came into contact with the knee of the man across from him. Gary turned back to their game. "It seems like I see these guys every other time I come in here. I don't know what they're doing but it sure looks like some kind of a drop to me."

"Right," laughed Chuck. "Right here in good ol' Superior, Wisconsin."

"It could be," countered Gary. He picked up his cue and prepared to make his next shot.

"Don't try to distract us when we've got some serious pool to play," added Randy.

Their game continued without further interruption. When Gary looked back to the front, he saw the three men leaving. The last man out the door had the package tucked snugly under his arm.

Chapter 11

2013, December 11, Wednesday

The snow was still falling although not as heavily as it had been. Nearly six inches of light fluffy powder had accumulated, coating everything with a bright clean blanket. The snow had arrived with almost no wind, which was unusual for this time of year, and so it piled up on the tree branches, fence rails, walls and any surface making puffy caps like peaks of icing on a cake. The plows were out clearing the streets making mounds at the crosswalks that pedestrians would breach with narrow pathways. Drivers who were unfortunate enough to leave their cars parked on the street would be coming back to find pushed-up barriers of plowed snow that only a good four-wheel drive or a snow shovel would overcome.

Cynthia had completed her classes for the day and was sitting in the student lounge. Her organic lab had involved the fractional distillation of cyclohexane and toluene, and that had gone extremely well. Gas chromatographic analysis of her samples had demonstrated both the improved effectiveness of her fractional distillation apparatus as well as the basic difficulty of achieving a complete separation. She was recording a few final observations in her notebook when Peter Dahle, wearing his usual chinos, dress shirt and sweater entered the room. "I thought I might find you here."

Cynthia smiled. Although her feelings for Peter were waning, and the recent development of her involvement with Rathburn presented complications that she didn't really want to face, she still appreciated his attentions. "Shall we hit the Caf?" she asked, gathering her belongings into her backpack. Bundled against the cold, the two traversed the freshly cleared sidewalks to the SC, stowed their coats and backpacks, and shuffled through the cafeteria line with the other students. The lunchroom area was brightly lit with stations for different types of food: burgers, pizza, salad bar, Asian food, taco stand, fruit juices, soda, and a soft serve ice cream machine. It was difficult to imagine that anybody could not find something to their liking, although complaints about the food were frequent topics of conversation among the students. When their trays were loaded, they found a table where they could sit together.

"How were your classes?" began Cynthia. "Let's see, what did you have today?"

"Ugh!" replied Peter, "I had Statistics this morning, and then the World Views perspectives course and then Business Models this afternoon. Business Models was the best. Jorgenson really makes it interesting. Makes me want to get out there and try something. I just need a gimmick."

"Cool," responded Cynthia. She enjoyed seeing Peter get enthused about an idea. However, Peter did not ask Cynthia about her classes. From past experience he knew that her descriptions of molecules, chemical apparatus, and physical properties would blow over his head and leave him feeling somehow inadequate. He liked it better when others were admiring him. Conversation lagged as Peter escaped into thoughts of owning and growing his own business.

When dinner was finished, they retrieved their coats and backpacks and began their trek home. The two occupied separate rooms in a rental house with four other students. The arrangement had been going pretty well. Most of the participants followed the house rules, being good about cleaning up after themselves, and keeping the noise level low. A few moments of friction had come up, but usually the disgruntled parties could escape temporarily to campus or another friend's place, so no lasting problems had developed.

Peter and Cynthia stomped up the broad wooden steps to the front porch of the house. Inside the front door was a convenient row of coat hooks on the wall and a tray for boots and shoes below. The interior was decorated with a faded patterned wallpaper and darkly stained woodwork. A stairway directly in front of them led to the second floor where there were four bedrooms. To their right was a large living room that boasted a window seat in front of a bay window and a fireplace that was boarded over and concealed by a large sofa. The living room opened into what used to be a formal dining room with ornate leaded glass cupboard doors above a sideboard. Behind that was a large kitchen. The landlord had wisely installed two refrigerators and a dishwasher. Two more smaller bedrooms were built into an addition that had been added on behind the kitchen.

Cynthia and Peter shed their coats and tossed their backpacks on the couch in the living room. Peter poked his head into the kitchen and they listened up the stairs, but nobody else seemed to be about. Turning to Cynthia, Peter approached her and attempted to take her into his arms. "I think we're alone," he said.

Cynthia allowed Peter to hold her, but her reluctance was apparent. She laid her head on his shoulder making her mouth unavailable for kissing. "We need to talk, Peter."

"What is it?" asked Peter backing away.

Losing confidence in what she was originally planning to say, Cynthia changed gears. "Have you ever heard of Ecstasy, Peter?

"Yeah, I feel it when I'm with you," he replied with a smile.

"No, silly. I mean the drug, 'Ecstasy', 'X', 'Molly'."

"Yeah, I've heard of it. I've done it a couple times. It's pretty cool."

"Ya wanna try some?"

"You mean you've got some?" Peter asked, his eyes widening.

"Yeah, a little," she replied with a touch of pride.

"Where did you get it?"

Cynthia looked at Peter for a moment. "I really shouldn't say. Okay? It's better if you don't know. Let's just say that if you need more, I can get you quite a bit."

Peter regarded Cynthia with a mixture of frustration at not being told and admiration that she was able to be connected enough to have access.

"You know that I work in a chemistry lab, right?" Cynthia asked suggestively.

"Right," said Peter. The wheels were churning in his brain. Thinking of his Business Models course, he imagined that if Cynthia could act as a supplier, he could easily find a ready market of students, young people with hormones, ready for adventure, who would be eager and willing customers. For the time being, he decided that he wasn't going to pressure her any further on her source, figuring that he would just let that be and see how things panned out. Still, he could not stop seeing dollar signs as he imagined all the ways that he could work this opportunity. As his thoughts drifted, Cynthia brought him back to Earth.

"Here," she said. She laid out two small glassine envelops on the coffee table. "Normally this would be mixed with some filler and packed into capsules, but this is the pure stuff. I just weighed out enough for one dose each. It doesn't look like much, but it doesn't take much. Just put a little water in here and drink the solution. Rinse it out and drink it again. That way you will get it all."

Peter did as he was told.

The following morning Cynthia awoke and pushed Peter's arm away. Finding a robe from among the clothes strewn on the floor, she proceeded to the kitchen. The clock on the stove read 10:10 and she was relieved to remember that she had no Thursday morning classes. She boiled water and poured it into a mug with a spoonful of instant coffee. With these seemingly monumental tasks accomplished she found a Pop-Tart, stuffed it into the toaster and blankly watched it until the hot treat bounced into the air. Sitting at the table, she studied the pattern in the Formica, nibbled at her breakfast, and sipped the ersatz coffee. She was almost finished when Peter, looking seriously bedraggled, appeared in the doorway. "Morning?" he offered uncertainly.

Cynthia nodded solemnly. Peter followed Cynthia's pattern, brewed some instant coffee and toasted a Pop-Tart. Across from each other at the table, the two sat in silence. Finally Cynthia spoke, "I've got something to tell you, Peter."

"Oh?" he replied, sensing the seriousness in her voice.

"Yeah. I'm going to move out."

At first he was completely puzzled, but then he felt the anger begin to rise. "What? Move out? Where? Why? What are you talking about? What's going on?"

"I've got a deal on a nicer apartment. I'll be moving in there the first of the year."

"Well, that's fine. Is there room for me?"

"No. And you should know, I'll be moving in with somebody else."

Peter regarded this with mixed shock and disbelief. "Somebody else? Like who?"

"Nobody you know," replied Cynthia. She didn't want to tell Peter about Rathburn, but wasn't sure how she was going to get around this questioning that was sure to arise. Peter was looking at her, the anger apparent in his face.

"But Cyn," Peter pleaded, "what about last night? What about all the good times we've shared? Are you throwing that all away?"

Cynthia looked back at him, feeling some sympathy for the anguish he was experiencing. "I've got to move on, Peter. You and I can't continue. We are going in different directions. We've been having fun, but that's all it is. We have no future."

Peter looked at her and shook his head. "I don't believe this. What are you telling me? Have you been seeing somebody else? Huh? What the fuck? Who? Who is it?"

Cynthia studied the coffee cup in her hands to avoid Peter's glare. Getting no reply, he stood up and kicked his chair to one side. "You, bitch! You, bitch!" With one look over his shoulder he left the room. Cynthia continued to sit at the table and listened to Peter in the bedroom upstairs rummaging through the closet and banging on various objects. Eventually she heard him descend the stairs and slam the front door.

"Okay," she breathed, "That's done."

Chapter 12   2016, April 8, Friday

Dr. Martinelli's eight o'clock advanced organic lecture had been just as animated and stimulating as ever, and the students, saturated with wonder and new knowledge repaired to the student assistants' lounge in search of respite and coffee.

"Where does she get all that energy so early in the morning?" asked Gary.

"I think she stores up potential energy overnight and then converts it to kinetic when she gets us in her classroom," retorted Jamie.

"Kinetic, definitely!" Gary replied.

"She gives real meaning to 'excited state'," added Andy.

"And 'activated complex'," suggested Kayla.

As they enjoyed their jokes and relaxed at their desks, a growing commotion outside in the hallway drew their attention. Going to the doorway they were just in time to witness a small parade approaching. At its front came Dr. Rathburn in his neatly pressed trousers, brightly polished Oxfords and tweed sport coat walking beside the squat Campus Safety Officer, Steven Davis. Behind them trooped two figures covered shoulder-to-toe in white HazMat suits trundling a dolly that held two large blue plastic barrels. Dr. Barton brought up the rear. Students in the hallway parted to let them pass as they headed toward the research lab. Lisa and Andy and a few other curious students fell in behind as the procession made its way down the hall. As unobtrusively as possible, Lisa and Andy followed them into the lab where they could see one worker winding up the yellow tape while the other snapped pictures of the blown-out hood sash, the smashed apparatus inside the hood and the floor area in front. The workers used eyedroppers to suck up liquid that still pooled in places on the floor of the hood, and squeezed these samples into labeled bottles. Small pads were used to wipe down other selected areas and these were similarly placed in labeled plastic bags. Then the damaged hood sash was removed from its track and placed on the dolly. They scooped up the glass shards and remnants of chemicals and equipment with dustpans and dumped the broken bits into one of the blue barrels. When cleared of debris, the interior of the hood was sprayed with some liquid solution. Absorbent pads were used to soak up the washings and these were stuffed into the second blue barrel. Finally, the floor in front of the hood was treated in the same way until the whole area had been completely cleaned and all evidence of the explosion was removed. All the while this was going on Lisa could see Barton, Rathburn and Davis huddled together beyond the workers, watching and speaking in low tones. When the job appeared to be finished, one of the workers presented Davis with a clipboard. Davis signed the bottom of the page and returned it, and the whole entourage reversed its course and trundled the dolly to the elevator at the far end of the hallway.

"Well, we won't find any more evidence there," commented Andy looking at Jodi's empty and newly cleaned work area.

"Yeah, that's for sure," agreed Lisa, turning away and heading toward the door. Then she added, "I wonder how Jodi is doing?"

Andy contemplated Lisa's thought and nodded, but then decided to change the subject. "Are you still up for the concert tomorrow night?" As part of a series of entertaining events that the Student Activities Board scheduled throughout the year, a rock band was on the program to perform in the SC the following evening. As a student-sponsored event, the tickets were fairly cheap, and it was likely to draw in a good portion of the student body.

"Yeah," agreed Lisa, "that'll be fun. But aren't you all going to the job fair in Minneapolis tomorrow?"

"No, no," answered Andy. "That's next weekend."

"Well," Lisa smiled, "In that case, I'm all for it. Will you pick me up?"

"Absolutely. Do you want to eat at the SC and then go, or do you want to eat somewhere else?"

Lisa considered the question and then replied. "We could study in the library tomorrow afternoon. Then going to the SC would probably make the most sense. Unless you have something more romantic in mind, Mr. Treydon," she added with a wink.

Andy brightened at the implication. "I'll see what I can do," he said trying to do a quick mental tally of his current financial holdings.

Later that afternoon the hubbub of activity was abating in the Science Building as the majority of classes were over for the day. Lisa, Mariah, Gary and Kayla were gathered in the student assistants' room resting from the concentration they had expended in their courses and labs, but not yet ready to start working on the assignments that were due the following week. Kayla was idly twirling a lock of her hair and sipping soda from a can while Gary was tossing popcorn into the air and catching it in his mouth.

Lisa found herself returning to thoughts about possible causes of Jodi's explosion. "Mariah," she began, "Cynthia Collins also works for Dr. Rathburn, doesn't she?"

"Yeah," replied Mariah.

"Have you seen her around? I almost never see her in here." Lisa waved her hand at a barely used desk off to one side.

"Yeah. She seems to just come in for classes and occasional lab time. I hear she has a fancy off-campus apartment."

"Do you have her cell-phone number or her address?"

"Yeah. It should be here." Mariah went over to Cynthia's designated desk and opened the top drawer. An identification card was taped inside. Mariah read off the information while Lisa copied it into her cell phone. She tapped the number and waited.

The phone was answered by a languid "Hello?"

"Hey Cynthia, this is Lisa Ross. Ah, I was wondering if I could talk to you a bit?"

"Yeah sure. What about?"

"Well, it has to do with Jodi Sander's accident. But I'd rather talk to you in person. Would that be okay?

"Sure, I guess." Cynthia didn't sound particularly interested.

"Ah, are you on campus now?"

"No, I'm at home."

"Will you be coming back today?"

There was a pause. "No, not today."

"Would it be okay if I come to your place?"

Again, there was a pause, Lisa thought she heard voices in the background, then, "Yeah, sure, I guess. Do you know where I live?"

"Ah, no." Cynthia gave her the address. "Okay, hold on just a sec." Lisa lowered her phone and looked around the room. "Andy's probably still in lab," she surmised. Spying Gary who was casually talking to Kayla and Jamie, she approached him. "Gary, could you give me a ride over to Cynthia's apartment?"

Gary looked at Kayla who shrugged. "Yeah, I can drive you," he replied. "I'd like to see her place."

Lisa spoke into her phone. "Alright. I'll be there in about twenty minutes."

Lisa and Gary walked to the east side commuter lot. Lisa had known Gary for only about a year. He had appeared in chemistry classes at Burlington as a junior, apparently having transferred in from some other school. As an older student, Gary presented a reserved but friendly exterior, keeping mostly to himself. Lately he seemed to be hanging out with Kayla more than any other student, but Lisa was not aware that their relationship might be anything more than casual. He typically wore a dark green military-looking jacket, hiking boots, and a black watch cap, and now Lisa observed that his mode of transportation was an aging military green jeep.

"So, Gary, where were you before you came to Burlington?" she began. I know that you must have transferred in here, right?" she added, trying to soften the bluntness of her question.

Gary regarded her for a moment. "I was in the Army and then I did two years of community college in Duluth."

"Oh," said Lisa, considering for a moment how she would regard this. "That's cool."

Gary looked at her sideways as they walked. "You think so?"

"Well, yeah. You were serving our country. I respect that."

They walked on in silence for a while.

"So why did you decide to come to Burlington?" Lisa asked.

"Well, I was in demolitions in the army. And I thought that was pretty interesting. So, when I got out, I wanted to learn more about explosives, how they're made and how they work and stuff." Then he added, "They really are pretty cool, if it isn't happening to you."

Lisa contemplated this and then considered Jodi's explosion. "Do you have any idea what might have caused Jodi's explosion?"

Gary shook his head. "I have no idea what she might have been working on. Unless she happened to be using an ether solvent that was contaminated with peroxides. That's always an issue one has to be careful about."

Lisa considered Gary's suggestion. "If we could only see her notebook, we would know if that was a possibility."

"Yeah," Gary agreed.

Gary's jeep barely had room for Lisa in the passenger's seat. The back seat was a jumble that made Lisa secretly question whether Gary might be living out of his car. Empty soda cans, cardboard boxes, a blanket, some wadded-up clothing and some crumpled wrappers from fast food restaurants littered the seat and floor. She decided that he must be residing elsewhere since there wasn't enough room for a human body the way it was.

Cynthia's apartment was located in a part of Superior known as Old Central Park. Historically this was the area where the wealthier denizens, lumber barons and shipping magnates, had built their mansions. A sprawling block of lawn, trees, a pond and paths was surrounded on three sides by large Victorian houses that looked out over Lake Superior to the northeast. Behind these, the neighborhoods became less and less prestigious where the merchants and then the dock workers had built their homes. Gentrification had removed many of the more run-down dwellings which were replaced with apartment buildings and boutique retail shops. The taller of the new apartment buildings commanded grand views of the lake over the tops of the historic mansions and the park.

As Gary approached their expected destination, he suddenly slowed his jeep and pulled over. "Look," he said pointing to the street in front of Cynthia's building. "Isn't that Rathburn's car?"

Lisa was less adept at recognizing automobile models but had to agree that the sporty red car parked on the street did look a lot like what she knew Rathburn drove. Sure enough, while they idled there, a man who looked like Rathburn exited the building and slid into the driver's side of the red car. With a glance up and down the street, he rapidly sped away.

Lisa and Gary looked at each other quizzically. "What would he be doing at Cynthia's apartment? Do you think…?" The thought was left unfinished.

Gary waited until Rathburn's car was out of sight and then pulled into the vacated parking spot. The two found her apartment number on the keypad under the canopied entryway. They buzzed her number and waited. A garbled voice came through the speaker followed by a loud buzzing as the door was unlocked. The elevator took them to the eighth floor where they found Cynthia's apartment to be only one of four on that level. Their knock was answered immediately. Cynthia was barefoot and appeared to be wearing only a white terrycloth bathrobe. Her hair was wet, as if she had showered recently.

"Come on in," she said with muted enthusiasm. To the right, the foyer led off to a kitchen area behind an island with bar stools. To the left was a rather formal-looking dining area. Straight ahead a large thickly-carpeted sunken living room furnished with several couches and a coffee table opened before them. A large flat-screen TV occupied one wall, while the adjacent wall was a bank of floor-to-ceiling windows that offered a breath-taking view of Lake Superior. Non-descript music was emanating from speakers somewhere.

"Not your average student apartment," breathed Gary to Lisa.

Cynthia led them into her living room and extended her arms. "Welcome to my pad," she said. "What do you think?"

"Wow, Cynthia. This is fantastic!" said Lisa. "What a beautiful view."

"Yes," she agreed, "my little perk." Cynthia stood beside them at the window watching the twinkling lights coming on as evening settled over eastern Duluth in the distance. "And now my two friends are here," she said looking at them. "So, what's up?" She flopped down onto one of the couches.

Gary and Lisa sat on the adjacent couch. Lisa began, "Cynthia, the reason for our visit is that we are trying to figure out what might have caused Jodi's explosion."

"Oh, yeah," said Cynthia, seeming to grow more sober at the thought.

"And I guess that I am feeling a little guilty, you see, because she asked me to check her notebook for her just before it happened, but I didn't get there in time."

"Uh huh…"

"So, we are thinking that if we knew what she was working on, we might have a clue what might have gone wrong."

"Yeah, I 'spose," she agreed.

"But, nobody seems to know where her notebook is," Lisa offered, watching to see Cynthia's reaction. "It's nowhere in her lab area."

"Well, I'd expect that Charles, I mean Dr. Rathburn has it."

"Yeah, well he says he doesn't," asserted Lisa.

Cynthia made a wry look. "Well, I doubt that he would tell you if he did. He is really protective of everything that he and his students do for SynZac. And he can just be ornery sometimes, so I'm not surprised if he doesn't want to tell you. He's probably afraid that you would find out something that would make him look bad."

"Well, directing Jodi to do something that results in an explosion is pretty bad, wouldn't you say?" interjected Gary.

"Well, yeah, I gotta agree with that, but I really can't help you. I don't know where her notebook is."

"Do you have any idea what kind of a reaction Jodi might have been working on? Do you know whether she was using an ether solvent?" asked Lisa.

Cynthia seemed to think about this for a moment, then shook her head. "Sorry. I really don't know. Jodi and I sometimes would consult with each other if one of us was repeating a procedure that the other had already done. But at other times we were doing stuff that was completely different and unrelated. I have no idea what she was doing last Tuesday."

Feeling like her trip to visit Cynthia was getting her nowhere, Lisa tried another approach.

"Well, can you tell us anything about what you do for Dr. Rathburn?"

A smile flickered across Cynthia's face, and she gave a small cynical laugh, but then her mood seemed to darken. She shook her head slowly back and forth. "Ya know, Lisa, you put me in a hard position. I'm really not supposed to talk about that with anybody. It's stuff for SynZac, and I'm supposed to keep it secret."

Lisa mulled this over. "Yeah, I suppose so." Then she added, "So there isn't anything that you can tell us that might help?"

"I'm sorry. I really don't know what Jodi might have been doing."

Unable to think of anything more to ask, Lisa looked at Gary and gave a slight nod toward the door. "Well, thanks anyway, Cynthia. You sure have a lovely apartment." They turned to go.

"Yeah, well, thanks. Maybe you should come back some time when you want to have some fun."

"Yeah, thanks. See you Monday morning."

Gary and Lisa rode the elevator to the ground floor in silence. Back inside Gary's jeep they sat and looked out the front window.

"That was useless," said Lisa. "I wonder where she gets the money for that fancy apartment?

"Don't know," said Gary as he started the engine and shifted into gear.

"And what was Rathburn doing there?" she asked. "Could he possibly be living in the same building?"

"Could be," said Gary.

"Well, she sure was clear about not wanting to tell us what either she or Jodi is working on," said Lisa. Then she added, "But I think that she knows. She just isn't telling us."

"Yeah, I think she knows what Jodi was supposed to be doing, but I don't think she knows what caused the explosion. I was watching her. I think that she is just as puzzled about that as we are."

"Yeah, maybe so."

Gary drove back to campus as the last light of day was fading over the western hills.

Chapter 13

**2016, April 9,
Saturday morning**

A background hum from various fans and pumps greeted Andy's ears as he entered the Chemistry Department's dedicated instrument lab. This room was cleaner than most of the laboratories. No chemical reactions or processing was conducted here. The room was used exclusively to house the variety of modern electronic instruments that were routinely used for the analysis of chemicals. The danger of ruining an expensive electronic tool necessitated keeping the instruments away from the labs where chemicals were mixed, and solutions were poured and stirred and boiled. Once a new chemical was isolated, then small, discretely measured and encapsulated samples would be brought into the instrument lab for their careful introduction into one or more of the specialized instruments.

After recovering the SPME fiber from Jodi's hood two days ago, Andy had carefully screwed it back into its bottle and placed it securely in his desk drawer. Now he stood before the GCMS, Gas Chromatograph - Mass Spectrograph, instrument and punched in a temperature program on the keypad. After pressing several buttons, he inserted the SPME fiber into the sample port and pressed the green start button. Andy moved to sit in front of the computer monitor on the adjacent desk and watch as the screen refreshed every few seconds. A bright green line began to trace across the dark screen. Suddenly, the line jumped to the top of the screen and then somewhat less quickly returned to the bottom. "That's just air," thought Andy, knowing that the act of opening the sample port to insert his SPME fiber would allow a small amount of room air to enter the instrument. Andy waited while the instrument ran through its gradually rising temperature program. Four more times the green line rose toward the top of the screen and returned to the baseline. After about thirty minutes no more compounds seemed to be eluting from the column. Andy decided that he had gotten all the material he was going to get from his sample and pressed the red "stop" button.

As the instrument cooled down, Andy examined the peaks that the green line had traced out, and moved the computer mouse to guide the cursor on the screen. As the cursor moved over the different peaks, a second screen window displayed spectra that consisted of forests of vertical lines. For each of the four peaks that his sample had produced, Andy collected a screen shot of each of these mass spectra. He selected an option from the "Print" menu, and hard copies of each of the spectra whirred out of a printer in the center of the room. Andy studied each one and jotted several numbers in a notebook. He logged off the computer and put the GCMS into sleep mode.

Back at his desk in the student assistants' lounge, Andy studied the spectra that he had just printed. With a cheerful "Hello" Mariah Jackson strolled into the room and dumped her books and backpack onto her desk. "Hey Andy, whatcha workin' on?"

Andy swiveled in his seat but continued to look at the spectrum in his hand. "There seem to be four major components to the vapors in Jodi's hood," he said. "I get molecular ion peaks at 60, 75, 150, and 207. But I'm not very good at interpreting the rest of the fragmentation patterns. So other than the molecular weights, I'm not at all sure what these represent."

Mariah stared at the wall thinking for a minute. "Sixty, 75, 150, and 207, …." she said slowly. "Well, I can tell you this," she stated with confidence, "the 207 component is the combination of the second two minus 18. So, I'd guess that the 75 and the 150 are the reactants and the 207 is the product, and the reaction involves a dehydration," she finished proudly.

Andy looked at her with admiration. "Very nice, Mariah. Wow. I bet you're right."

Mariah was on a roll. "One more thing," she added, "very likely the 75 component contains nitrogen, and that is probably also present in the product."

"Dude!" Andy exclaimed. "How do you know?"

"The molecular weight is an odd number," Mariah answered smiling.

"Mariah, thank you. You're brilliant. This is really going to help." Andy turned back to his desk and made several notations in his notebook, while Mariah started organizing her desktop. They each busied themselves at their desks in silence for several minutes. Finally Andy turned again toward Mariah. "I still am going to need help to interpret these spectra."

"Talk to Dr. Martinelli," she suggested. "She's really good at that stuff."

Andy nodded in agreement. "Thanks." He carefully placed the spectra in a manilla folder in his backpack, pulled out a text for a different class, and settled down to read.

Later that evening, after a meal at Rocky's Ribs Restaurant in downtown Superior, a meal that was not especially elegant, but nevertheless quite different from the fare at the UC, Andy and Lisa joined up with Gary and Kayla inside the main atrium of the SC. They purchased their admissions and wound their way between tables until they found a location on the balcony that overlooked the stage and dance floor. Lisa and Kayla sat while the men went to fetch chips and drinks from the possibilities at the mocktail bar.

Standing in line, waiting to place his drink order, Andy noticed Cynthia standing alone and sipping a drink off to one side of the room. He left his spot and went over to greet her. "Hey, Cynthia. How's it going?"

Cynthia turned to look at him and smiled. "Andy, my old bud." She slipped one arm around his waist and gave him a half hug. That familiar move brought memories back to Andy. It had been the first week of college when the freshman had come to campus before all the other students. A variety of activities had been planned to familiarize the students with the physical layout of the campus and the different departments and offices that they would be expected to navigate as they progressed through the curriculum. Social activities had been planned as well, including a dance at which Andy and Cynthia had met. The two of them had entered the ballroom at the same time, and so had struck up a casual conversation as they both stood surveying the floor. Knowing nobody else, Andy had invited Cynthia to dance, and she had accepted. They had spent much of the evening together, and toward the end they had stepped outside onto a balcony to admire a view of the campus mall. In the cool darkness of the shadows, Cynthia had snuggled up to Andy and slipped an arm around his waist underneath his sport coat. Andy, in his usual state of loneliness, was overcome by Cynthia's forward display of affection.

Completely willing to accept her attraction to him, Andy enveloped Cynthia in his arms and kissed her. She kissed him back with eagerness and kissed him again. Her body was pressed against his and he could feel the contours of her thighs and chest. They continued to hold each other and kiss for several long minutes until they both needed to stop for breath. Finally, holding hands, they went back into the dance, and later Andy had walked Cynthia back to her dorm and said goodnight. In spite of that promising beginning, they had not pursued their relationship. Although they ran into each other on campus from time to time, and were sincerely friendly, neither one of them seemed to want to pick up where they had left off after that one passionate encounter.

Now that Cynthia had come up and given him that half-hug, all the memories came rushing back. Andy still thought that Cynthia was attractive, but he felt vaguely troubled and confused by the affection that he felt. "Hi, Cynthia," he greeted her, "are you here with somebody?" He looked around.

"Naw," she replied.

They stood for a moment without speaking and watched the stagehands push equipment around on the stage. Then Andy went on, "We don't see you around the student assistants' lounge very often. We all kinda assumed that you were going with somebody." Andy hoped that his statement would be taken as a question.

Cynthia thought for a moment. Then said, "Well… I kinda am. But he isn't anybody who would come to something like this." She motioned at the stage. "I really like these guys' music, so I had to come by myself. Don't worry about it."

Andy understood that she didn't really want to discuss it and was happy to let her have her privacy. Realizing that he had a drink order to collect, he made a move to leave. "Good to see you, Cyn. I hope you have a fun evening." They smiled at each other, and Andy stepped back into the drinks line.

Andy got back to Lisa and the others just as the main attraction was assembling. Much hoopla accompanied the appearance of the band called "The Yorkie Shorts" on the stage. Four brawny and bearded young men whose claim to fame, apart from their rendition of predominantly Celtic-themed music, was their wearing of kilts. The rumor that they liked to promulgate was that none of them wore underwear beneath their kilts, but it had never been proven one way or the other. Nevertheless, they received a warm and enthusiastic welcome from the audience and proceeded to reward them with some very loud and rhythmic music. Soon the area in front of the stage was alive with students, mostly jumping up and down and waving their arms back and forth in the air.

"Shall we?" Gary asked Kayla.

"Yeah, let's," she agreed rising from her chair.

"Will you guys watch our stuff?" Gary asked Andy and Lisa.

"Sure thing," Andy agreed. Happy to have a suitable excuse not to mix with the bouncing crowd below, Andy turned his attention to Lisa. He scooted his chair closer beside hers and reached over and took her hand. They sat there for a while sipping their drinks, listening to the music and watching the throng below. Suddenly Andy sat forward. "That's Gary's friend down there, isn't it?"

"Who?" replied Lisa.

"Peter Dahle, and, no, I know he is not really Gary's friend. I don't think that they get along very well at all, really," Andy added. "What's he doing?"

While most of the students on the floor below were swaying or jumping with the music, Peter, wearing a sport jacket over a white shirt with a narrow dark tie, was leaning against the wall off to one side partially surrounded by a small cluster of male students. Although the darkened room and the flashing lights made seeing anything a bit difficult, it was apparent that, from time to time, a student or two would separate from the crowd and approach Peter. Each would take something out of their pockets, an exchange would take place, and the students would depart. This continued for a while until the stream of students declined and Peter and his coterie moved off toward one of the exits. "That looks interesting," said Andy, sitting back.

"Do you think he was selling something?" asked Lisa.

"I doubt that he was giving away candy," said Andy.

A while later Gary and Kayla returned to their chairs, flushed from their exertions on the dance floor. "Whoosh!" said Kayla, flopping onto her chair and grabbing her drink.

"They sure can drive a beat," said Gary. "You guys doing okay up here?"

"Yeah, we're fine," replied Andy. "We saw your favorite guy down there. Peter Dahle."

Gary shook his head dismissively, "Definitely not my favorite guy." Then he added, "Listen, we're going to take off." He slurped the last of his drink and pushed his chair back.

"Okay," said Andy looking at Lisa. "I think that we are going to hang a little longer." Andy and Lisa watched Gary and Kayla depart and then remained, sipping their own drinks and enjoying the music.

Later that evening, on the sidewalk outside, Lisa took Andy's arm as they walked across campus in the direction of her house.

"I got a letter from the University of Minnesota today," Lisa announced quietly.

"Oh yeah!" Andy responded. He knew that this was likely to be about Lisa's application to graduate school. "What did it say?"

"I'm in," she stated, still quietly, but with a definite tone of pride.

"Oh, Lis! Congratulations!" Andy stopped, held her at arms' length and then enfolded her in a big embrace. They resumed walking and things were quiet for a moment. "So, you are going to be in Minneapolis next year," he mused. "Do you know when you'll be moving?"

"Not for sure," Lisa replied. "My rental contract here goes until the first of August, so I don't have to be out until then. But in the meantime, I'll need to find a place in Minneapolis before September, so whenever that starts, I'll be able to move. But otherwise, there is nothing to keep me here after graduation. If I move back in with my parents in St. Paul, my dad might find me a summer job in his law office, but I'm not sure that would be much fun. I have no idea if I could find something menial around here." Images of waitressing at a restaurant in Duluth's Canal Park came to mind. "Or if I'd want to," she continued. "It would be kinda nice to travel, or just take some time off."

"Well, I'm going to go to that job fair next weekend and look for something in the Minneapolis area," said Andy. He turned to look at Lisa and said, "I'm really hoping that you and I will be seeing each other in… in… in the future."

The two faced each other on the sidewalk in the dark. "I want that too, Andy," said Lisa. Let's see what we can do to make that work out. Okay?"

"You've got my promise," said Andy as he put his arms around her and kissed her. They stood in the dark, holding each other and kissing. Finally, they broke apart and continued their walk to Lisa's door in silence. Andy waited as Lisa went up her porch steps.

"I'll call you tomorrow," called Andy. "Let's go to the library, okay?"

Lisa smiled and nodded. "See you then."

Andy turned and walked the familiar sidewalks from Lisa's door to his. He thought about the feelings that his encounter with Cynthia had aroused, and then the feelings that Lisa's news had aroused. And then the big question of how in the world was he ever going to secure what he wanted for his own future.

Chapter 14

2016, April 11,
Monday afternoon

Her inorganic analysis lab over, Lisa found Kayla in the student assistants' lounge sitting at her desk chewing at the tips of several strands of her hair and half-heartedly looking at a textbook. Kayla's cheerful disposition was always a welcome presence in a variety of social groups on campus. But now it was Kayla who welcomed the distraction that Lisa presented, and greeted her as she came in. "Yo, Lisa, howzit goin?"

"Okay," replied Lisa, flopping into her chair. She sat and stared without speaking for a moment.

"You want to go with me to visit Jodi in the hospital? I haven't heard how she's doing in almost a week."

"I'm sure we'll all hear when she's better," offered Kayla.

"Yeah. I know. But I'm going to go visit anyway. Her mom and dad looked so dejected when I was there last time. I think they appreciate knowing that Jodi's friends care about her."

"Okay," Kayla said, closing her books. "That did it. I'm coming."

Lisa and Kayla walked the few blocks to Lisa's rental house where she had a garage stall. Although Lisa's parents were happy to supply Lisa with her own automobile, a new white Toyota Avalon, Lisa wasn't fond of driving, and preferred to beg a ride from friends when she could. However, she knew that Kayla, coming from a less well-to-do family, did not have access to a car except ones others provided for her. While Lisa's father was an attorney working for a firm in downtown St. Paul, Minnesota, Kayla was from Hayward, Wisconsin where her folks owned and worked a corner restaurant. Differences in social class were unimportant to either of them and they enjoyed their time together.

Lisa drove cautiously up Tower Ave. and turned into the hospital parking lot. Without stopping at the reception desk, she led Kayla directly to the fifth-floor patient rooms. They paused at the doorway to Jodi's room and peeked inside. As before, it was dimly lit. Only Jodi's mom, Linda, was sitting beside Jodi's bed. She seemed more haggard than before and startled as Lisa and Kayla stepped into the room. "Hello," called Lisa softly.

Finally recognizing Lisa, Mrs. Sanders urged them to come in.

Lisa introduced Kayla, and they moved quietly around Jodi's bed. Jodi still lay there unconscious, with glowing numbers winking on the bank of instruments above the headboard. "How's she doing?" asked Kayla.

"Oh, about the same. The doctors aren't sure why she doesn't wake up. They say that the brain scan looks okay, and it looks like there won't be any lasting damage. She seems to be okay, but she just isn't awake yet."

"You must be getting tired," Lisa said to Mrs. Sanders.

"Oh, my, yes," said Linda. "Don had to go back to work, so he left on Sunday. Fortunately my sister lives in Duluth so she has been able to get to Cloquet to look after Jodi's younger brother and sister. Oh, I just wish this would end." Linda sat on her chair and looked at her hands.

"We are all so sorry," offered Kayla, "We keep hoping that, that, well, Jodi will get better. We'd love to see her back at school."

Linda seemed to perk up. "Thanks so much for coming to visit. It is so comforting to know that Jodi's friends care about her." Continuing on, she added, "it was also nice that her professor and that man from the University Safety Department came here, too."

"Really?" asked Lisa. "Professor Rathburn and Mr. Davis?"

"Yes," she replied. "They have both been here a couple of times. They don't stay long, but they have stopped by. They seem very anxious to see Jodi when she wakes up."

Lisa and Kayla looked at each other and considered this.

"Do either of them tell you anything about why they thought the explosion occurred?" asked Lisa.

Linda shook her head. "No. I asked once, but they said they didn't know. They just kinda pop in. Look around, ask how she's doing, and then go. It seems sort of, well, brief," she said looking a bit puzzled. "Sometimes they come in together," she added.

"Huh," was all Lisa could think to say.

Lisa and Kayla moved about the room pretending to look at the sparse decorations, and then moved back to stand at Jodi's bedside. When they couldn't think of anything more to do or say, they nodded to each other and started for the door. "Well, it's been nice visiting with you," offered Lisa. "We'll be in touch."

"Goodbye. Thanks for coming."

Lisa and Kayla couldn't shake off the weight of the mood from Jodi's room as they made their way to the elevator.

Chapter 15

Lisa threw off her covers, hit the stop button on her alarm clock a good fifteen minutes before it was set to go off, and pulled on jeans and a sweatshirt. After a quick bite of toast and orange juice, she donned her coat and pulled on her boots that she paused briefly to admire for their curious fractal-like white stains of winter salt. She shouldered her backpack and set off for campus. Her apartment on 18th street was a short five block walk from the science building located near the north end of the campus. The skies were clear, the air fresh and invigorating. The day would likely warm to temperatures in the forties, or maybe the fifties, and the students would respond by appearing all over campus in shorts and t-shirts as if they were living on a tropical island. After the long northern Wisconsin winter, even the slightest taste of warm weather was cause for celebration. For the moment, however, Lisa was glad to have her insulated boots and long puffy down coat.

On her walk toward campus, Lisa thought of the chemical-soaked paper towels that she and Andy had collected from the site of Jodi's explosion. Andy had showed her the results of his mass spectral analysis. He had found four components of different molecular weights, and Mariah had offered a couple of suggestions that would probably be very helpful, but they still needed more evidence, a more complete analysis. Lisa thought about how she would try to isolate the components of Jodi's reaction from the towels that they had recovered. "This procedure isn't one that I will find in the lab manual. I've got to figure this out myself," she thought. The idea gave her a feeling of pride and excitement. "I can do this," she thought. "I know what I'm doing." She considered the different techniques that she had used in past lab courses and in her research project. "I guess that the logical move would be to extract them," she thought. "But which solvent should I use?" She envisioned the bottles of chemicals that awaited her in the solvent cupboard.

Lisa dumped her coat and books at her desk in the student assistants' lounge and slipped into the sneakers that she kept there. She donned her lab coat and crossed the hall to the research lab where she found the room unoccupied. "Hah. First one in. Just as well," she thought. "Nobody to bother me or ask nosy questions." The site of Jodi's explosion now looked bleakly empty and clean. At her fume hood she uncovered the bucket of paper towels that had been used to clean up some of the mess from the explosion. The acrid odor of acetic acid was strong. She donned her safety goggles and rubber gloves and used a pair of tongs to remove one of the contaminated towels and wad it into a large beaker. "I should probably use a medium polar solvent," she thought as she considered the row of bottles in the solvent cupboard. She poured a quantity of ethyl acetate over the towel in the beaker and agitated the contents for a few minutes. She repeated this procedure with the other towels and combined the ethyl acetate extracts. She draped the processed towels over the edge of her bucket to dry and put this back in her hood. Next, she filtered the resulting solution, shook it together with several portions of an aqueous base solution, washed and dried it, and filtered it again. She placed the resulting final solution in a round bottom flask and attached it to a rotary evaporator. Within a few minutes Lisa had a small amount of a viscous yellow liquid in the bottom of her flask. "Okay," she thought as she held up the flask and rolled it back and forth. "What do you contain? You are going to tell me," she said softly to the thick golden liquid fluid.

"First, let's see how many components are in there," she thought. Lisa used a thin pipette to remove a single drop of the liquid, placed it in a small vial and diluted it with a few drops of acetone. Then she used a fine glass capillary to dip into this solution and deposit small dots of this liquid on a white silica chromatography slide. She placed the slide in a glass chamber containing a shallow layer of solvent and waited patiently while the liquid in the bottom of the chamber rose slowly up the slide by capillary action. When the liquid had reached almost to the top of the slide, Lisa removed the slide and waited for the small amount of adsorbed solvent to evaporate. She took the slide to a small dark chamber and turned on an ultraviolet light. The slide glowed a brilliant green color except for two dark spots that Lisa marked with a needle. "Well, there are at least two components," she thought. "But that might not be all. I'll try one more trick." Back at her bench, she scanned a row of spray cans on the shelf. "Maybe permanganate will reveal something," she mused. Selecting one of the cans, she placed the slide at the back of her hood and sprayed it with a short burst. Instantly the slide changed to a bright magenta color. The two spots that she had marked earlier turned brown and these were accompanied by a third brown spot farther up the plate. "Aha," she thought, "three components, at least." Satisfied, she sat back and studied the slide. Looking back at the golden liquid in her flask, she thought, "Okay. Step one."

The sound of footsteps alerted Lisa that someone was approaching. She was pleased to see that it was Andy walking toward her. "I thought I'd find you here," he greeted her.

Lisa smiled at him, hoping that she was conveying both her relief and her real fondness for his presence. "I've been extracting some of these towels," she said pointing at the bucket. "And I think that I've found at least three components."

Andy looked at the thin layer chromatography slide with the marked spots. "I have at least one component worked out," said Andy. "I think we can be pretty sure that the solvent Jodi was using was acetic acid. First of all, it reeked of it there," he said pointing in the direction of Jodi's hood. "And second, it would correspond to the m-over-e peak of sixty in the mass spec that I ran."

Lisa nodded in agreement. Then she added, "I used a base wash step when I did the extractions, so I hope that all the acetic acid has been removed from the material that I've isolated." She held up her round bottomed flask to show Andy the bit of liquid.

Andy took the flask, removed the cap, and waved his hand over the opening, wafting the air toward his nose. "I'd say that you have gotten rid of it, alright."

Lisa nodded.

"So, what are you going to do next?"

"Well," began Lisa, "I've been thinking..."

"Oh-oh!" Andy interrupted grinning. "We know what happens when you do that."

"Hush!" scolded Lisa. Continuing on, she said, "We won't know much about these three components unless we get them separated, so, I guess a column would be the best way to do that. Then it would be nice to see some spectra on each of them."

"Sounds good," agreed Andy. "What solvent will you use?"

"I got a nice separation on TLC using five percent ethyl acetate in hexanes, so I think I'll stick with that."

"Do you want any help?" asked Andy.

"I'd love it."

Andy stepped out of the room for a minute and reappeared wearing his lab coat and goggles and carrying a box of small test tubes that he began dropping into slots in a plastic rack. The racks in turn were arranged side-by-side on the deck of an automated fraction collector. Meanwhile, Lisa assembled a tall glass column containing a white granular powder and clamped it to a metal pole over the fraction collector. The bit of liquid that she had previously isolated was mixed with a small amount of solvent and injected at the top of the column. A small mechanical pump connected to a large jug delivered solvent through a flexible tube to the top of the column. As drops of solvent dripped from the bottom of the column into one of the test tubes in the racks, the automated collector made a quiet whirring sound and clicked as it periodically shifted from one tube to an empty one. All the while, a computer screen displayed a bright green line tracing across the screen that would periodically rise toward the top of the screen and then fall back down to the baseline.

Andy stood behind Lisa as they both watched the tubes fill with liquid one-by-one and the colored trace of the chromatogram build up across the computer screen. Andy gently placed his hand on Lisa's shoulder. "This looks good," he commented. "'Looks like you've got good quantities of all three components."

"Yeah," Lisa agreed. "We're going to get this." She leaned her head against Andy's hand, momentarily enjoying the comfort of his support. She stopped the pump, hit "Save" and "Print" on the computer, and began disassembling the column. The racks of test tubes were moved to her fume hood. Tubes containing the same component were poured together into round bottomed flasks and concentrated on the rotary evaporator. Finally, Lisa and Andy were looking at three small flasks each containing a small amount of oily liquid. A layer of argon gas was blown into each flask, and they were sealed with yellow plastic caps.

"I'm going to have to stop for now," said Andy. "Lunch is calling to me."

"Sounds good. May I join you?" Lisa replied.

"Of course."

The two shed their lab coats and made the short hike to the SC. The day had warmed up beautifully. The smell of sodden earth newly released from melted snow permeated the warm air. As expected, students wearing less than sensible amounts of clothing were congregating around picnic tables and playing frisbee.

Shunning the main cafeteria in the lower level of the SC, they each selected a plastic-wrapped sandwich and a bottle of soda from the mini-mart cooler. A small table next to a balcony overlooking the main cafeteria afforded a view of the milling students below as well as a view of the campus mall through tall two-story high windows. After eating in silence for a few minutes, Lisa asked, "Do you have any time this afternoon? I'd sure like to see the spectra on those products we got."

Andy put down his sandwich. "I've got P-Chem Lab from two to five today. And I've got to do some review before that starts. But it doesn't always require that I stay the whole three hours, so I may have some time later this afternoon."

"Me, too," nodded Lisa. "I'm assisting in an organic lab at the same time. We almost always run long. Maybe I can find you around five o'clock and see what's up. I'm dying to see those spectra."

"Yeah," he agreed. "Barton is pretty protective of his NMR. Will that room be unlocked after five p.m.?"

"I don't think that they lock it up until the Campus Safety officer comes by later on. I'd guess that's around nine or ten. I've been able to get on the instrument some evenings in the past."

Andy nodded. Then Lisa added conspiratorially, "Besides, now we know where Mariah keeps her key." They finished their sandwiches and moved off to a lounge where they settled into some large softly upholstered chairs and reviewed their notebooks for the coming classes.

Later that evening the two returned to the research lab. Back in her work area, Lisa eyed the three flasks of oily liquids that she had isolated earlier. Andy paused at Lisa's fume hood and examined the bucket holding the towels that Lisa had processed earlier. "Lis," he began, "what's this white stuff?"

The paper towels that she had been extracting earlier had dried out and now were covered with a fine powdery white coating. "I have no idea," she murmured as she looked more closely at the towels.

Using a metal spatula, she scraped a little of the white powder off one of the towels and brushed it onto a square of glassine paper. She spooned a small amount into a short test tube and added a few drops of water from a squirt bottle. Instantly the white powder dissolved.

"I bet it's inorganic," she said. "It must not have dissolved when I extracted the towels with ethyl acetate. So, it was left behind when the towels dried out."

Andy nodded in agreement. "So now we have one more component to identify, then, huh?"

"Great," said Lisa. She carefully unfolded each paper towel and dusted the white powder onto a large glassine paper. Finally, the collected powder was placed in a small vial and labeled.

Returning to the unknown liquids that they had isolated earlier, they prepared samples for spectroscopic analysis. First, Lisa assembled three narrow glass tubes and filled each with a solution of one of the unknown components. These were carried to the instrument lab where they were inserted into plastic cylindrical holders and placed into the autosampler for the Bruker 400 MHz nuclear magnetic resonance spectrometer, known to chemistry department personnel as the NMR. At the computer console, Lisa typed in the commands that started the sampler. The snake of sample holders moved along the mechanical track; the arm lifted the sample and placed it gently into the opening in the center of a large cylindrical magnet about the size of a washing machine. With a hiss from a jet of air, the sample disappeared from sight as it descended into the magnet. Lisa typed a sequence of commands and within a few minutes a series of sharp spikes appeared on the screen. After a few more keystrokes, a paper copy of the spectrum was printed, and Lisa signaled the autosampler to change to the next sample. Finally, Lisa had three printed NMR spectra in hand. She retrieved her sample tubes from the autosampler and went back to her desk in the student assistants' lounge.

Meanwhile, Andy had taken a drop of each isolated component and applied them one at a time to the attenuated total reflectance sample stage of the Bruker infrared spectrometer. Several keystrokes at the computer console likewise resulted in three printed infrared spectra sliding into the output tray of the printer in the middle of the instrument lab. Andy cleaned the sample stage, put the spectrometer in sleep mode, and joined Lisa in the lounge.

"Okay, Lis," Andy began, "with, IR, NMR and mass spec we should be able to nail these." They began to study the spectra of each component in turn.

"Well, this one can't be hard. There is only an ethyl group in its NMR," said Andy pointing at a cluster of peaks on the page.

"Yeah. Ethyl and what else?" commented Lisa.

"Whoa. Look at this IR spectrum. Big nitro peaks."

"Nitroethane? Let's see." Lisa did some mental calculations. "C2, H5, N, O2, …aah 75. It would have a molecular weight of 75."

"Bingo," said Andy. "We have a component with m-over-e of 75 in the mass spec."

"Okay. One down," Lisa smiled.

Andy continued to look at the sheets. "But is nitroethane the cause of Jodi's explosion? It isn't really explosive, is it?"

"I don't think so…" Lisa looked doubtful, and slowly turned to the next set of spectra. "Look at these other two NMRs. There is definitely something in the aromatic region in both of them."

"This component has this small peak way down here at 10 delta. Do you think that's an impurity?"

"Let's see," muttered Lisa. "That component also has a carbonyl peak in the IR. Isn't that where aldehydes show up?"

"Yeah, I think so." Andy flipped open a textbook and started sliding his finger down a numbered chart. "Yup. Aldehyde."

"So, if we have a benzene ring and an aldehyde, that would account for about 106 or 105 in the mass spec. What is the next molecular weight we are dealing with?"

"One hundred fifty." answered Andy.

"So, we have a mass of about 44 or 45 to explain."

"Yeah," Andy trailed off while they both flipped from spectrum to spectrum and jotted diagrams and numbers on scraps of paper.

Then Lisa began to bounce in her chair. "Oh, Oh, I think I've got it. Look, the integration indicates only three hydrogens on the ring, so in addition to the aldehyde there are two more substitutions. And there is this sharp singlet that integrates for two. That could be a CH2 with no neighbors. So, how about a ring of -O-CH$_2$-O- on the benzene?"

Andy drew a new diagram, sat back and nodded. "That would work. But what would the substitution pattern be?"

Lisa reexamined the NMR spectrum and pointed to the peaks in the benzene region. "Look at the coupling. These two are adjacent, and this one is alone. So, it is like this." She pointed to the diagram that she had recently drawn.

"I think you've got it. Well done, Lis." Andy looked back and forth from the diagram to the spectra, nodding. Picking up the third set of spectra he placed them side by side on the desk before them. "Mariah brilliantly pointed out that the molecular weight of the third component is a combination of the other two minus a molecule of water, so we should be able to figure this one out right away." Andy drew the structure of nitroethane and the substituted benzaldehyde on a piece of scratch paper with a plus sign between them and an arrow pointing to the right. "So, what would we get from these two?" he mused.

The two of them, sitting close together and hunched over Lisa's desk, examined one spectrum and then the other and the diagram of the reaction. Muttering comments to each other, they gradually constructed a diagram that represented the product. When they finally had their solution, they sat back and rechecked the facts indicated by the spectra against their proposed structure.

"Well. I think we've got a good answer," said Andy, "But does it help us to explain Jodi's explosion?"

"I don't see it," said Lisa shaking her head. "Yeah, we have a couple of nitro groups, but those don't automatically make something explosive."

They sat looking at their drawings and calculations until finally Andy flipped his book shut and got up. "Well, I've got to go. We have Martinelli's class tomorrow at eight, and I've got a little more work to do before then." Then he added, "Would you like me to walk you home?"

"Yes, I would," Lisa agreed and began stacking up the spectra and their notes. They collected their backpacks and coats and walked the length of the corridor to the stairwell.

Outside the night was dark and the temperature had once again fallen below freezing. But the thin coating of snow and ice had melted off after the warm daytime sunshine, so the sidewalks were pleasantly clear. They talked of coming tests and assignments in their classes and the possibility of some entertainment on the impending weekend. Outside the door to Lisa's rental house, they stopped, and Andy turned to face Lisa. "Have a good night, Lis," he said and bent forward slightly and kissed her on the lips.

Lisa kissed him back and attempted to hug him as well as their coats and backpacks would allow. Then she paused and looked Andy in the eye. "We do make a good team, don't we?"

"Yeah, I think so," agreed Andy.

"Yeah, me too." She smiled and ascended her porch steps. "See you tomorrow."

Andy waited until the door had closed behind her.

Chapter 16

2016, April 13, Wednesday morning

The next morning Andy, Lisa, Gary, Kayla, Cynthia, and Mariah were seated near the front of the classroom where Dr. Lydia Martinelli was explaining how to predict the stereochemical outcomes of pericyclic reactions. Dr. Martinelli was slight in build, standing about five foot six. She wore dark-rimmed glasses and kept her short dark hair neatly trimmed. This day, she had on a black dress and wore a red patterned scarf at her neck. The ideas that she was trying to explain were esoteric, but her enthusiasm for the subject and her dynamic presentation kept her fairly flying back and forth in front of the whiteboard where she drew figure after figure in hopes that enlightenment could be imparted to her charges. The students were riveted, at least in wonderment of her apparent excitement with the subject, if not for the subject itself. When she finally concluded, they all breathed a sigh of relief before packing up their notes and backpacks. A few minutes later they had reassembled in the student assistants' lounge, sipping sodas or coffee, and delaying their settling down to prepare for their next classes.

Lisa pulled out the file folder that contained the spectra that they had acquired the night before. She flipped it open, looked at the first spectrum and the proposed reaction diagram, and walked over to Andy. "I'm going to ask Mariah and see what she thinks of this." Andy nodded in agreement and followed Lisa over to the desk where Mariah was flipping through the pages of a thick textbook.

Lisa recounted to Mariah how just before the explosion Jodi had asked her to check her work, how Jodi's notebook had gone missing, and then how she and Andy had collected samples from Jodi's work area and extracted and identified the four components. Mariah nodded in approval as she listened to Lisa's description of their chemical analysis. Finally, Lisa presented the drawing representing the chemical reaction that Jodi must have been conducting.

"We think that we have figured out what she was doing, but we don't understand why this would have led to an explosion. Can you help us?"

Mariah looked at the diagram, looked at each of the spectra, and then looked back at the diagram. Finally, she set the papers down and looked at Lisa and Andy. "Was Jodi doing this on her own?" she asked suspiciously.

"Well, I don't think so. I guess I don't really know. Officially she works for Dr. Rathburn."

"Rathburn," Mariah said with a sour look. "And now her notebook is missing, you say."

"Yeah," replied Lisa, "and when I went to ask him about it, he basically told me to butt out and mind my own business."

"Which you didn't do," Mariah added, looking askance at Lisa and smiling.

"Well, no," replied Lisa, feeling only a little guilty.

Mariah fingered the spectra and looked again at the chemical diagram. "Do you have any idea what this is?" she asked lifting the diagram so that they could see it.

"Not particularly," replied Lisa. "I just assumed that it was something for his contract with SynZac."

"Not likely," responded Mariah. "This is a first step in a classical synthesis of amphetamine. Usually there would be some additional base in there such as sodium acetate. But you're right. There is no real explosion hazard that I can see in what you have shown me here." Mariah set the papers aside and appeared to be ready to table the subject when she picked up the chemical diagram with renewed interest. "Let's see…" she muttered and began drawing something next to Andy's drawing. "So. If you completed the synthesis, this is the substituted amphetamine that you would get." She held up the paper with a new chemical diagram on it. "Do you know what this is?" she asked.

Lisa and Andy glanced at each other and shook their heads.

"Make some of this and you would have a nice batch of the stuff they call 'Ecstasy'." She paused while Lisa and Andy registered her meaning. "I have no real idea what this stuff sells for on the street, but a half kilo of this should be worth quite a lot."

Awestruck, Andy and Lisa stared at Mariah and then looked at each other. "How do you know this stuff, Mariah?" asked Andy.

"Well, you know that next year I'm going to graduate school in pharmacology, right?"

"Yeah."

"So, I've just been studying up on some of the more interesting drugs that are out there." She waved a hand at a large textbook lying at the back of her desk. "Besides, they talk about some of these drugs in the neuropsych class they teach in the Psychology Department."

Andy nodded in appreciation. "Nice!"

Again Mariah asked, "So, do you think that Jodi was making this on her own?"

Andy and Lisa looked at each other again and shook their heads. "Jodi making Ecstasy? To sell?" asked Lisa. "No. No way. I don't believe it. That's not like her at all."

"She wouldn't do that," agreed Andy. "I doubt she even knew what this was. She must have been doing this under Rathburn's direction."

"Which raises the question of what is Rathburn up to," added Lisa. The thought hung unanswered. Momentarily Lisa looked at her phone. "Oh, hey, I've gotta go. Dif EQ." Lisa went to gather her things and departed while Mariah turned back to her textbook.

Andy went to his desk and pulled out his notebook for his next class. After a few minutes perusing his old notes, he found himself struggling against a flagging will to do anything academic. He turned his chair and looked around the room. Jamie Perrin was at his desk, hunched over a textbook. Gary was sitting on Kayla's desk doing his best to distract her. And a rare sight, Cynthia Collins was at her desk, apparently finishing up whatever she had been working on and stowing some items in a drawer. Andy got up and walked over to her. "Hey Cynthia. What's up?" he asked casually. "Did you enjoy the Yorkie Shorts last Saturday?"

"Yeah," she brightened and turned to face him. "They were a lot of fun." Then she added, laughing, "we almost got to see McKnelly's secret, right?" She was referring to some of the band members' antics on stage that had resulted in one member's kilt getting lifted almost high enough to reveal the answer to whether he went "commando".

"Yeah," Andy agreed. "But I don't think that they will ever really let us know." Then, observing Cynthia's research notebook spread out before her, he asked, "So what are you doing today?"

"Just getting ready to run a reaction," she answered. Noticing his gaze, she gently closed her notebook.

"Do you like working for Rathburn?" he continued, trying to keep the conversation going.

She looked at Andy suspiciously. "It's okay," she replied lightly. "I get to do quite a variety of things; I'm getting a lot of experience," she added with a shrug. She gave him a faint smile but picked up her things and headed for the door.

"Cool," he replied softly, watching her go. Andy still wasn't sure why he and Cynthia hadn't become better friends. He thought that Cynthia was pretty and that he would have liked to have gotten to know her better. But she always seemed to hold everybody at arm's length. At least, their interactions were always cordial. He wondered whether anybody knew her well.

Chapter 17

2016, April 14,
Thursday morning

Lisa awoke with the sunlight pouring in through the curtained windows of her bedroom. Relishing the fact that she did not have any eight a.m. classes that morning, she snuggled under her wool blanket and quilt, avoiding the cooler areas of the bed just beyond her cocoon of warmth. She thought of Andy and the pleasant times they spend together and wondered what it would be like to have him lying next to her now. She imagined reaching over and touching his bare chest, his turning toward her and lying face to face, his reaching for her, touching her… there. "Oh, yes, that would be nice, yes," she thought. But then the thought that her breath might be stale and that she really needed to pee invaded her consciousness. Crashing back to reality, she threw off her reverie with the covers and headed to the bathroom.

From the kitchen table she could hear some of her roommates stirring, doors shutting and showers running. She plodded through a bowl of Cinnamon Toast Crunch and sipped some coffee that was still hot in the coffee maker. With assignments due in three of her classes on Monday, her time for the rest of the week was looking pretty occupied. She hadn't specifically planned a time to meet Andy at the library, so she punched in his number on her cellphone.

"Hello, lover boy," she said coyly when he picked up.

"Oh, ah, Susan? Stephanie? Monica?" he replied playfully.

"Yeah, right," she growled. "Hey, Andy. Two things. Do you want to meet at the library today? And would you drive me up to the hospital to see Jodi before that?"

"Yeah. That'd work," he replied after a pause. "I'm assisting in a gen chem lab this afternoon, but I could go this morning. We could get some library time after we get back."

"Okay, how about in half an hour?"

"Alright. See you out front in thirty."

Once again, they found themselves speeding south on Tower Avenue toward Memorial Hospital. Andy turned his car into the now familiar lot and started looking for an open space.

"Oh. Look at that," exclaimed Lisa softly. Two figures standing at the end of the sidewalk outside the entrance were talking animatedly. Professor Rathburn and Steven Davis appeared to be in the midst of a fairly heated discussion as it was apparent that voices were being raised and fingers pointed in the direction of the hospital. Andy pulled into a parking spot and turned off the engine. They sat and watched the two figures until their argument subsided, and they departed in separate directions.

"I wonder what that was about?" mused Andy. "It doesn't look like they are getting along very well."

"Hmmm," said Lisa. "Maybe Rathburn wants to hide the fact that he, or rather Jodi, was making Ecstasy in the lab. If Jodi wakes up, he doesn't want her to tell Davis and get him in trouble. Maybe?"

"I guess… maybe," he replied.

They proceeded to the elevators off the lobby without stopping at the reception desk. As they walked the quiet hallway toward Jodi's room, their thoughts turned once again to the seriousness of Jodi's condition. "What if she never recovers?" thought Lisa. Thinking of all the hopes and dreams that she had for her own future, Lisa felt a great sadness as she imagined Jodi being deprived of all of her aspirations. Pausing at the door to Jodi's room they knocked gently and started to push the door inward. Abruptly the door was pulled open from within and Mrs. Sanders stood there looking much fresher than she had previously. Instead of inviting them inside, she stepped into the hall pulling the door partially closed behind her. "Hello Lisa, and, uh, Andy, right?" she greeted them.

"Yes. Hello, Mrs. Sanders," they replied.

Before they could ask further, she went on brightly. "She's woken up!"

"Oh my gosh," enthused Lisa trying to look around Mrs. Sanders into the room. "That's great."

"Yes, yes. But, I've got to tell you. I'm afraid that she doesn't remember anything. She didn't know her own name at first. She barely even recognized me," she added sadly. "But she is making progress. Some things are coming back. The doctors think that this is very hopeful. They're going to start some physical therapy with her."

"Oh, that's great," said Andy.

"We are so happy for you," added Lisa, "and Jodi, of course. Can we see her?"

"Well, yes. That's why I came out here to talk to you. She probably won't remember you. So, I just wanted you to be prepared for that. Okay?"

They nodded, and Mrs. Sanders pushed the door open. Inside they found Jodi sitting up in bed with a magazine in her lap. Together they moved to the far side of the bed.

"Hello, Jodi. How are you feeling?"

Jodi looked at them quizzically. Mrs. Sanders quickly intervened, "These are two of your friends from school, Jodi. This is Lisa, and this is Andy."

Jodi nodded and looked pleased. "Hi. Nice to meet you," she volunteered easily.

Lisa decided to dive in. "I guess you aren't remembering us, but we used to hang out together at Burlington U. We are all majoring in chemistry, so we've taken many of the same classes and work in the same department. So, yeah, we've been friends for quite a while."

Jodi nodded, but then shook her head. "I'm sorry, but I'm still feeling pretty lost. I wish I could remember you better. Some things are coming back, though slowly."

Lisa glanced briefly at Mrs. Sanders wondering whether her next question would be okay. "Do you remember anything about the explosion that injured you?"

Jodi just shook her head. "So far I only seem to be able to remember some things from long ago. I remember growing up in our house in Cloquet. I remember Mom and Dad and my sisters, and some things we did many years ago. But anything recent doesn't seem to be there."

"Wow," said Andy under his breath.

"Well, you just hang in there." Lisa took Jodi's hand and patted it. "I bet that they will be able to help you get better. And then I hope that we will see you back at school. Okay?" Lisa hoped that she wasn't sounding overly optimistic.

Lisa and Andy talked about how their classes were going and events that were happening on campus while Jodi appeared to be paying attention. When they could no longer think of things to say they started to move toward the door. "Well, take care, Jodi. We hope to see you back soon."

"Thanks for stopping by," she called after them.

Mrs. Sanders followed them out into the hallway. "That Professor was here again this morning, with that safety guy," she began. "They're kind of strange, don't you think?"

Andy and Lisa paused. "How's that?"

"Well, first of all they seemed rather surprised or even upset that Jodi was getting better. Then, they don't seem so interested in how Jodi is feeling as to whether she remembers what she was doing in the lab when the explosion occurred," she explained. "They kept asking her."

"Yeah, that does seem pretty strange," Andy and Lisa agreed. "Well, goodbye for now, Mrs. Sanders. We'll be back in a few days to check up. But this sure does look like real progress for Jodi."

Once Jodi's door was closed, Andy muttered, "Rathburn should know damn well what Jodi was doing. He was the one who gave her the instructions."

They returned to Andy's car, but before he could turn the key in the ignition, Lisa put a restraining hand on his arm. "Andy. We've got to do something. We're getting nowhere."

"What do you mean? Where are we going?"

"Look. We think that Jodi was making drugs for Rathburn, right? Something went wrong and there was an explosion. And now her notebook is mysteriously absent. This is not right, and we should do something."

"Do something? Like what? What can we do?"

Lisa paused, not entirely sure what her answer would be to that question. "Maybe we should go to the police," she said tentatively.

"Really?" Andy checked the time on his phone. "The police? How long is that going to take? Do you think we have enough evidence? I mean…"

"I don't know. But we are Jodi's friends, and we are the only people that know that something suspicious is going on, and nobody else seems to be doing anything about this."

Andy slumped in his seat and thought about the things he had planned to do before his lab at two p.m. His motivation to do anything was at low ebb at the moment, but his interest in being Lisa's partner in whatever she was doing was considerable.

"Well, okay. Now?"

"Yes. Let's go now. I can't wait."

The location of the Superior Police Department was at 12th and Hammond. After circling their destination, they found an on-street parking spot a couple of blocks away. They donned their coats and walked the last few blocks. The day was bright and cold and brought a flush to their cheeks as they traversed the neat downtown sidewalks to the light-colored stone building. Following the signs, they proceeded around one side of the building and entered on the basement level. The lobby's stone floor felt cold. A few plastic chairs with metal armrests were arranged to one side. Directly in front of them a very solid-looking glass window with bars and a small grill for speaking protected a portly middle-aged woman in uniform from anybody or anything that might happen in the lobby. To one side there was a steel grey door that clearly announced, "Authorized Personnel Only".

Approaching the window, Lisa addressed the woman, "We would like to talk to a police officer."

The woman eyed her seriously. "What's the nature of your business?" She seemed to be writing something, but neither Lisa nor Andy could see what.

"We think that we know of a crime that is, or has been, committed. And we want to tell somebody."

The woman stopped writing and again looked at them without smiling. Then she seemed to relax, rubbed her eyebrow, and looked at a chart off to one side. "Okay…okay…. Alright. Please have a seat. Somebody will be with you shortly."

Andy and Lisa sat on the stiff chairs and examined their surroundings while they waited. After a few minutes a man wearing dirty clothes and much in need of a haircut, a shave, and a bath came in and followed a not-so-straight path to the window. "I've got shum important imformashun," he proclaimed loudly to the woman behind the grill.

They heard some voices behind the window and then the steel door opened and a large man in uniform came out. "Come on, Charlie," he said gently grasping the man by the elbow. Charlie seemed familiar with this officer. "I tell you, you're gonna wanna know what I've sheen."

"Okay, Charlie," the officer said steering Charlie toward the door. "You can tell me outside. Alright?" The officer pushed open the door and escorted Charlie up the steps.

Andy leaned over to Lisa and whispered, "I hope we get a better reception."
Lisa scoffed quietly.

As the burly officer and the rumpled man departed, the door next to the glass window opened again and this time a handsome young officer with blonde hair stood in the doorway and looked around the waiting room. Realizing that Lisa and Andy were the only two there, he addressed them, "Are you the folks who want to talk to an officer?"

"Yes," answered Andy getting up.

"Hi. I'm Chris Jenkins. If you'll just follow me back here, we can sit down and talk."

The two followed Officer Jenkins down a hallway into a very bleak, nearly empty room. A steel table was positioned in the middle of the room with two chairs on either side. Andy noted that the legs of the table were bolted to the floor. One wall of the room featured a large black rectangle of glass. "A one-way window?" thought Andy. "It's hard to imagine that anybody would consider us worth watching."

Officer Jenkins indicated a couple of chairs where they could sit. "Would either of you like some water or coffee?" he asked, but then lowered his voice and added, "But I really wouldn't recommend the coffee."

"No, thanks, officer," Lisa replied.

"So. First of all, could I please get your names?" He opened a small notebook and took a pen out of his shirt pocket. Andy and Lisa provided their names, their home addresses, campus addresses and phone numbers. Then he looked up and smiled. "So, what's this all about?"

Lisa began. "We think that one of our professors at Burlington is involved in making drugs in the lab. Ecstasy. And we think that somehow he was responsible for an explosion that injured one of our classmates."

"Hmmm..." Jenkins responded making notes in his book. "And what makes you think this?"

Lisa proceeded to describe the results from the analyses that they had done and told of their thwarted efforts to find Jodi's missing notebook. Andy sat by nodding and occasionally injecting a supporting comment. When they had finished, Jenkins closed his notebook, replaced his pen in his pocket, sat back in his chair and folded his hands on the table.

"Okay, here is what I can tell you. First of all, thanks for coming in. It is important for our society that we have good citizens who are alert and speak up when they see something that they don't think is right. However, the Burlington campus has its own safety and security department, and the Superior Police Department normally does not go onto the campus unless they are invited. So, for any issues that might involve criminal activity or even perceived criminal activity on that campus, one should first go to Burlington's own internal police department.

Okay? However, something like illicit drug manufacturing is likely to eventually find its way off campus, and then it becomes our business. So, I'm glad that you came and told us. I am going to do some checking, and we will probably contact the Campus Safety Officer at Burlington. We will make note of your suspicions and keep a watchful eye, but we won't do anything about this until we get a request from their department, or if the criminal activities spread to outside their boundaries. See how that works?" He looked from Lisa to Andy.

They sat quietly for a moment and digested what Jenkins had said. "So that's it?" asked Lisa.

"Yup. At least for now," agreed Jenkins. "We'll be doing some investigating into what you've told us, and we'll be calling Mr. Davis. Then we'll decide whether any further action is warranted."

"Well, I guess we're done here then," said Lisa. She stood and collected her coat from the back of the chair. Andy rose behind her and followed as Jenkins opened the door and led them back to the lobby. "Again, thanks for coming in. We appreciate being alerted to this."

Outside on the sidewalk Lisa squinted in the sunshine. "Well, that didn't get us very far, did it?"

"No. And I'm not real excited about going and talking to that Davis guy either," commented Andy. "He's anything but friendly."

"Yeah, I know what you mean," agreed Lisa as they turned and headed back to Andy's car.

Chapter 18   2016, April 15, Friday

The next morning as Dr. Martinelli was wrapping up her eight a.m. organic lecture, Andy got to his feet and addressed her. "May I have a minute to speak to the class?" he asked.

"Certainly," she responded as she collected her notes from the podium.

From the front of the room, Andy addressed the class. "I think everybody here knows about the STEM job fair in Minneapolis tomorrow; I've already spoken to many of you. As you know, Jamie will be driving his van and if there is anybody else who wants a ride, there is still some room. Anybody who rides is expected to chip in for the gas, of course. In addition, Jamie's parents live in a suburb of St. Paul and they have offered to feed us all supper on Saturday night and put us up for the night as well. Jamie and I will be figuring out in what order he will be picking people up tomorrow morning, so if you all would put your address and phone number on this sheet…" he held up a notebook, "then we will text you and give you an approximate time to be ready in the morning. It's all going to start around five a.m., and, of course, some of you will be earlier than others. Okay? Thanks." He passed the notebook around as the interested students wrote down their relevant information and exited the classroom. Cynthia was the last to sign the notebook.

"I'm glad that you'll be riding with us, Cynthia," said Andy softly as he watched her write.

Cynthia looked at him as if to say, "Really?", but gave him a faint smile nevertheless.

"See you tomorrow," Andy called as Cynthia gathered up her things and departed.

⚗

Later that afternoon, the building was growing quiet as students finished their activities and departed from the campus. Mariah, dressed in black sneakers, black leggings and a loose black boat-necked top, stood in the doorway of the student assistants' lounge, hands on hips, and looked around. "Where is everybody?"

Only Kayla was at her desk collecting some papers and arranging them in her backpack. "I think most of them are off getting ready for the job fair tomorrow," she suggested.

"Oh, yeah. Of course." Mariah walked over to Kayla's desk.

"Aren't you going?" Kayla asked, looking up.

"No. I've been accepted to the graduate program in Pharmacology at the U of M for next fall. No point going to a job fair."

"Nice," said Kayla. "Isn't grad school a lot of work? I can't imagine going to school anymore. I'll be glad to be out of here."

"Well, the science really fascinates me. I just want to know more. And I want to be able to do more with it."

"Well, good luck with that. I admire your ambition."

Mariah paused, and then asked, "Hey, Kayla, would you have some time to give me a little help right now? My parents are coming tomorrow, and I have a whole bunch of solutions that I need to prep for the freshman inorganic qual labs on Monday. I'm not going to have any time this weekend, so I've got to get it done tonight."

Kayla looked up. "Yeah, I guess I can help. Unlike some people I know, I got my resume finished and copied several days ago.

Mariah smiled at Kayla's reference to Gary's habitual tardiness. "Well, thanks. I'd really appreciate it."

Kayla finished packing her things and followed Mariah down the dimly lit hallway to the prep room. As an energy conserving measure, the lights in many of the University's buildings were dimmed automatically at times when it had been determined that few students or staff were in the building. The emptiness and subdued lighting imparted a spooky secretive feel to the halls that were normally bright and bustling with talkative students. The departmental prep room was a large room adjacent to the stockroom across the hall from several of the first-year student laboratories. Mariah showed Kayla to a bench where she could work and indicated in a loose-leaf notebook a list of solutions that were needed.

"How about if you do those, and I'll do these," she said pointing to two columns in the book. They set about collecting bottles of reagents from the shelves, weighing out quantities of various chemicals and mixing them with water in large flasks. Several liters of each solution were needed. Soon a variety of colored solutions were swirling on magnetic stirrers. When ready, these were poured into clear glass jugs and labeled with neatly printed stickers. For the most part, the two worked alongside each other silently, but then the sound of raised voices in the hallway drew their attention. Pausing in their manipulations, they walked closer to the door that was slightly ajar.

One voice was heard to say, "…yeah, but what if she wakes up and starts telling everybody about…" The rest was indistinct.

Then the other voice replied, "Well then you are just going to have to…" followed by more indistinct words.

The first voice came back a little more loudly, "You can't possibly expect that I am going to…" Again, the rest of the conversation died away as the speakers moved down the hallway. Kayla and Mariah edged closer to the door and peeked out. Light from the doorway to Professor Rathburn's office spilled out onto the floor. Thinking that she had recognized one of the voices, Kayla turned to Mariah, "Rathburn?" she whispered.

Mariah nodded and then whispered, "And?" She lifted her hands and shrugged.

Kayla returned the shrug. "Do you think that had anything to do with Jodi?

"I really have no idea," said Mariah. She turned back to her work and carefully printed "1.0 M Copper Sulfate" on a large label that she affixed to a jug of bright blue solution.

"Rathburn!" Kayla spat. "Why is it that everything he does seems suspicious or creepy?"

Mariah shook her head. "I know what you mean. Have you seen the way that he looks at the women students?"

"Yeah," Kayla agreed. "What a jerk."

Finally, all of the solutions were mixed and stored alphabetically on the shelves.

"Kayla, I think that you've done enough," Mariah said checking the instructions in her notebook. "I can take it from here. I'll just clean up and put these things away."

"You sure? That's all?"

"Yeah, Thanks so much for your help tonight."

"No problem," replied Kayla. "This was no trouble. I'm all ready for tomorrow. I think that the fair will actually be kinda fun. I'm really excited to think about where I might end up next year."

"Ah, are you and Gary going to try to, um, coordinate your plans in any way," asked Mariah cautiously.

"Yeah, well, we're kinda thinking about it. I'm really not sure what might work out. That issue is still rather unsettled, right now, I'm sorry to say."

Mariah nodded. "Well, good luck this weekend. I hope you get lots of offers."

"Thanks. We'll see." Kayla headed back down the hall to the student assistants' lounge.

Chapter 19

2016, April 16,
Saturday

The sound of his alarm at five a.m. jolted Andy from what had been a very pleasant dream, something involving Lisa and walking through a field of grass on a warm sunny day. Then he remembered why he had to get up so early and launched himself to an upright position. Thankfully, he had done his packing the night before and laid out his clothes for the day. He was happy to find that his sport coat didn't need cleaning; he couldn't remember the last time he had worn it. His white dress shirt was still as clean as it was when he came to campus at the beginning of the semester, and it took him three tries before he could get the ends of his necktie to come out even. Nevertheless, with a quick glass of orange juice and a bowl of cereal in his stomach, he was down on the street and ready to go in thirty minutes. Moments later, Jamie's maroon van swung around the corner and pulled up by the curb. Andy threw his small duffel in the back and got into the front seat beside Jamie. Looking around, he saw that he was the second passenger to have been picked up that morning. Cynthia was sprawled across the far back seat. "Good morning, Cynthia," he called.

A sleepy "Mmm hmm," was all he got in reply.

"Who's next?" he asked Jamie, who seemed quite wide awake and confident of where he was going.

"First Kayla, then Gary," he replied.

Andy sat back and watched Jamie navigate the streets of Superior. When all were aboard, Jamie headed north on Tower Avenue progressing onto I-535 over the harbor and then on to south I-35. The humming of the tires and the warmth of the van soon had everyone but the driver nodding off. Cynthia had gotten horizontal and seemed to be asleep in the back. Kayla was leaning cozily on Gary's chest and Andy was trying to find something to use as a pillow against the vibrating window next to him. An hour into the trip, the sun was coming over the horizon and lighting the pine forests that flanked the highway. Jamie announced, "We are coming up on Hinckley, folks. We'll be taking a few minutes here. I'm going to fill the tank, and if anybody needs the restroom, this is your chance. And, of course, Tobies is right there with its world-famous sticky buns."

Jamie pulled up to the pump and released his occupants into the crisp morning air. The passengers spilled out, stretched, and headed for the restaurant. Refueled and refreshed, they were soon once again speeding down I-35.

As they came into the Twin Cities, Andy activated the map app on his cell phone and guided Jamie through the labyrinth of Minneapolis' one-way streets. Finally, the dome of the convention center came into view. As they disgorged from the van in the center's parking lot, Jamie, who was looking quite spiffy in a classic navy-blue sport coat with a crest over the breast pocket, a polo shirt, chinos and penny loafers, addressed them all, "Okay, folks, when the party is over, we all meet right here by this entrance." He pointed to the large double doors into the convention center closest to where they were parked. "We might as well meet just inside where it will be warmer until we all show up. You all have each other's phone numbers, so if anything comes up, be sure to tell somebody. Okay? My folks are expecting to serve us dinner at six, so be here by five. Alright?" The students shouldered their backpacks and joined the stream of young people like themselves pouring in through the doors.

The interior of the center was alive with voices and activity. The central area was surrounded by booths each of which sported a large banner with the name of a company or organization and their logo displayed in bright colors. Tables and carpeting made each booth look as attractive and comfortable as somebody's living room. Representatives from the different companies were neatly dressed and eager to welcome the students who stepped into their domain. At one end of the floor was a series of tables with signs overhead announcing registration, and signs below indicating which portion of the alphabet would be served at each table. Students were lining up at these tables, checking in and picking times for interviews with the different companies. The center of the floor featured a large carpeted area with stuffed chairs, coffee tables and a table offering an array of free snacks and drinks. Around the perimeter of the room were more permanent concession stands where a variety of fast foods could be purchased.

As Andy stood in line waiting to register, he spied Gary and Kayla talking together in the next line over, checking the list of employers. "What am I doing here?" he wondered. "Everybody else here knows what they're doing. What do I know? Can I really do what any of these companies will expect of me?" He looked down at the folder containing copies of his resume in his hands. "Are they just going to laugh at me?" Then it was his turn at the table.

The neatly dressed smiling woman at the keyboard took his name and slotted him in for interviews at different times throughout the day. Andy walked away and looked at the slip of paper with his schedule on it. Feeling as if he were jumping into a lake without knowing where the bottom was, he thought of his mother. In spite of the trials that she had had to deal with after his father had left, she had always been Andy's champion. After long days at work, she would come home and give him a hug, ask him how his day had been and prepare a good meal. She took time to listen to him and helped him think about the choices and challenges in his day. When he felt that he was facing some big difficulty, she never tried to downplay it. "Life is hard," she used to say, "but you do your best. If you are going to try, give it your all."

"Okay, mom. Here goes," thought Andy. He looked around the room for the banner advertising the first company on his interview list.

The morning passed quickly. Eager students moved from booth to booth, occasionally taking breaks and pausing by the refreshment table in the middle of the floor. Around midday, Cynthia found Andy standing looking at his phone. "How's it going, Andy?" she asked.

"Oh, hi, Cyn," he replied, stuffing his phone in his pocket. "Uh, okay, I guess."

She looked at him quizzically. "Yeah?"

"Oh, the interviews seem to be going okay, but Lisa isn't answering any of my texts."

"Hmmm," Cynthia responded. "Well, she's probably in the middle of something."

"Yeah, I 'spose," he muttered. Turning his full attention on Cynthia, he asked, "How about you?"

"Well, okay, so far. I had hoped to get an interview with Crane Analytical, but they were all filled up. I'm from Chicago, you know, and they are located down in Racine. It would be really nice if I could get something a little closer to home."

Andy scanned his schedule. "Hey, look. I grabbed an interview with Crane scheduled for 3:30. You could have it if they'll let us switch. You know that Lisa is going to be in Minneapolis next year, and I am really hoping that I might be someplace near there. If that is ever going to work out…" he trailed off.

Cynthia gave him a quizzical look. "Are you and Lisa making plans?"

"Well, maybe…" he responded with some reluctance.

She watched Andy struggle with his thoughts and shook her head. "Men," she muttered under her breath. Then, "Let's go see if we can reschedule." They headed for the registration tables.

As five o'clock neared, the group reassembled by the entrance. "Everybody ready?" Jamie asked. They were. They piled into the van and with Andy's navigation they were soon heading north out of Minneapolis on I-35. Jamie's parents lived in an exclusive suburb of St. Paul called North Oaks. As they turned into the central road, they were stopped by a guard at a gatehouse who let them pass when their destination had been identified and recorded. Jamie's passengers watched in awe as they wound their way along the boulevard flanked by wide green lawns, stately trees, ponds with swans, and large mansion after mansion.

"My god, Jamie, you live here?" Kayla enthused.

"Yeah. But don't be impressed. They're just houses. The people in them are the same as anywhere else. They watch the same television programs and buy their food in the same supermarkets."

"Uh-huh," she agreed. But they all continued to ogle their surroundings.

Finally, Jamie pulled into the driveway of a large brick colonial style house and turned off the engine. The front door of the house opened, and a handsome older couple came out to greet them. Jamie intercepted them. "Mom, Dad, these are my friends, Gary, Cynthia, Kayla, and Andy. These are my folks, Roland and Ellen." They greeted each other and shook hands.

"Come in. Come in," called Ellen, leading them into the house while Roland stayed to help Jamie and Gary unload backpacks and duffels from the back of the van. They trooped into the house and quietly marveled at the luxurious interior. Ellen showed them around and then led them to a den that was paneled in dark oak with overflowing bookshelves. Roland, with a tanned face, thick white hair and a soft yellow sweater draped over his shoulders, went to a bar in one corner. "Would any of you like a drink?" he offered. "I'm assuming you are all old enough, so if you aren't, don't tell me." He laughed at his own joke. "Besides, nobody is driving anywhere tonight, right?" Raising his voice, he called out to his wife in the kitchen. "Ellie, do you want some white wine?"

"Of course, Rollie," came her reply.

Soon they were called to the dinner table. As they assembled in the dining room, Andy checked his phone again for texts. Ellen was showing the students to their places, and, noticing Andy, she announced to the group, "And, we have a rule here, no cell phones at the table, okay?" The students dutifully silenced their phones.

The formality of the dinner was unfamiliar to the students. A white tablecloth, cloth napkins, two forks and a floral centerpiece contributed to an experience that was completely unlike any eating event that they had encountered at Burlington. Nevertheless, Roland and Ellen were jovial and soon the students felt at ease. Once everybody had been served, Roland spoke up. "I'd like to hear from each of you how your experiences went today. So, let's go around the room and take turns. Tell me what went well. And, if you want, what didn't go so well. Did any of you get an offer, or is everybody still waiting?"

They each took their turn, and soon the conversation was flowing, each relating their successes and gaffes. Andy felt that he had had one especially promising interview for a technical position with a professor at the University of Minnesota. Jamie ducked the questions saying that because he was a junior, he had made it known that he was not going to accept any offers for the coming year. Kayla and Gary both had positive feelings about interviews from two different companies, one in St. Paul and one in a Minneapolis suburb, but there were no firm assurances. When it was Cynthia's turn, she started by giving Andy a shy look. "Well," she said, "I got exactly what I wanted. I got an interview at Crane Analytical. That's in Racine, Wisconsin, where I would be really happy to locate. And they promised me that an offer would be sent to me in the next week." She smiled broadly and looked around the room.

"Well, done!" the others exclaimed. "Way to go, Cyn." And "Congratulations."

Cynthia looked at Andy, caught his eye and mouthed the words, "Thank you."

When dinner was done, they moved to the living room. It was decorated with plush light-colored carpet, multiple couches and chairs, end tables, and several very large oil paintings that seemed to all have a scenic rural theme. The students admired the surroundings and enjoyed the comfy chairs. Roland offered after dinner drinks but none of the students took him up. Finally, Jamie spoke up, "Mom, Dad, let's show these folks their rooms. We've got to be on the road pretty early tomorrow."

The students were shown to their accommodations. Cynthia and Kayla were each given separate bedrooms while Gary and Andy each had a couch in the den and the adjacent family room. Towels, pillows, and blankets were distributed and soon everyone was comfortably bedded down. Andy made one last attempt to text Lisa, but still there was no response. In spite of his fatigue, he lay awake in the dark for a long time before sleep would come.

Shortly after seven a.m., Jamie walked into the den and flipped on the lights. "Romp and stomp, it's daylight in the swamp," he called. The young men groaned and rolled over.

"No, no, not yet," Gary pleaded.

"Come on, guys. Breakfast is waiting."

Dressed and packed, they came into the brightly lit kitchen where they found the Perrin's housekeeper in a black and white uniform, standing behind a cooktop built into an island counter.

"What'll you boys have?" she asked. "Would you like bacon, sausage, eggs any style, toast, orange juice or coffee."

"Yes," said Gary appreciatively. Andy nodded in agreement.

They placed their orders and joined Cynthia and Kayla who were already seated and eating in a breakfast nook that was surrounded on three sides by windows overlooking a green lawn that sloped away toward a small creek. A few minutes later Jamie came in and joined them. "Thirty minutes 'til liftoff, okay?"

"No problem," responded Gary who was clearly enjoying his breakfast. But Kayla and Cynthia immediately got up, bussed their dishes, and left the room.

A little later they were out front, stuffing their belongings into the back of the van. Jamie hugged his mom and dad and climbed into the driver's seat. "See you next week," he called out the window as they started down the driveway.

The late April day was warm and bright. The snow was gone, and buds were greening on the trees. Andy sat quietly in the front passenger's seat and watched the scenery speeding by. "Where am I going to be next year?" he thought. Although a variety of possibilities were on the horizon, the uncertainty of it all was unsettling. And why wasn't Lisa answering her phone?

Chapter 20

2016, April 16,
Saturday morning

Try as she might, the sunlight streaming through the curtains of her second-floor bedroom window made it impossible for Lisa to go back to sleep. Although the others were away at the job fair, and she could've slept in if she had wanted, the light and her biological clock said it was time to be awake, and she just wasn't going to get any more sleep no matter how much she would have wanted to avoid the day. Besides, her mind was already humming with lists of things that she wanted to do. Springing out of bed, she went to the kitchen and put an egg on to boil. Nobody else was making a sound. "They can all sleep in. Why can't I?" she wondered. "The curse of an active mind," she answered for herself. While she kept one eye on the egg on the stove and got dressed, she also made a mental list of tasks for her to do when she got to school. Finally, fed, showered and dressed, she set off for campus. When she arrived at the Science Building, she ascended the steps rapidly until she came out in the hallway on the third floor. "Barely breathing hard," she thought to herself as she walked the length of the corridor to the student assistants' lounge. No surprise the place seemed emptier with many of the regulars away at the job fair. Some faculty were in their offices with their doors ajar, but the student labs were shut and locked, and for the most part the place was quiet. "Just the way I like it," she thought, "Time to get lots done." As the first to arrive in the student assistants' lounge, she switched on the lights and proceeded to her desk. With her books and notebooks arrayed before her, she eyed the coffee pot on the side table. "Later," she thought, and flipped open the first of her assignments.

An hour and a half later, a noise at the door drew her attention. Turning, she saw Mariah come into the room followed immediately by a handsome older couple. "Mariah, hi," she greeted her friend.

"Lisa, I'd like you to meet my parents," Mariah said indicating the two older people. Mr. Jackson was wearing a dark business suit and carrying his hat and a black overcoat. Mrs. Jackson wore an eye-opening purple overcoat with a large purse hanging from one arm.

"Very pleased to meet you," said Lisa standing and offering her hand.

Mariah's dad stepped forward and shook Lisa's hand. "Very pleased to meet you, too."

"How long are you in town for?" asked Lisa.

"We're just here for the weekend," volunteered Mrs. Jackson. "We'll be coming back for graduation in a few weeks, but we're going to take a load of Mariah's stuff home now, so we don't have to move it all in May.

Mariah continued, "Mom, Dad, Lisa is going to be at the U of M next year like I am. Except she'll be in the chemistry graduate program instead of pharmacology. Different schools, but not too far apart. We will probably see each other a lot."

Mariah's parents smiled. "That sounds very nice. I think that you both are going to be working very hard. We're proud of you."

"Thank you, Mr. and Mrs. Jackson. That's very kind. I do hope that Mariah and I can stay in touch."

Mariah's parents wandered about the room, casually examining the charts on the walls and the diagrams that had been left on the whiteboard. As they started moving in the direction of the door, Mariah came up to Lisa.

"Hey Lis, I gotta tell you. Last night Kayla and I were prepping solutions for the gen chem inorganic qual lab, and I got to thinking about that white powder that you gave me. Well, if inorganic qual is supposed to identify inorganic ions, why not give it a try? So, I ran it through the qual scheme that the students are supposed to do. And, dang, your compound is soluble in everything! Jeez! I started to worry that Kayla and I had made up the solutions incorrectly. So, then I think, 'What ions are soluble in everything, well, at least among the common counterions, that is?' Well, the answer is…" she counted on her fingers, "one, ammonium, and two, nitrate. So, listen, I add a little base to your compound and sure enough, it smells of ammonia. Score one. The second ion was a little harder. There is a test for nitrate, but it is a little complicated, so I cheated: I used spectroscopy. But that confirmed it. Your nice little white powder is ammonium nitrate." Mariah held her hands out to the side, palms up. "Ta daaa."

"Mariah! That's amazing." Lisa gaped at her. "Wow, you did it." But as she thought further, she darkened. "But does that explain anything? About the explosion, I mean."

"Well, maybe," began Mariah.

"Really?"

"Possibly. So, first of all, that condensation reaction that Jodi was doing would normally require a mild base such as sodium acetate. Ammonium nitrate doesn't qualify at all in that regard. So, it makes no sense for it to be in there. If Jodi put it in, it was either her mistake or a mistake by whoever told her to put it in. Second," she paused and looked at Lisa narrowly, "Do you know what ammonium nitrate is used for?"

Lisa drew a blank. "No, can't say that I do."

"Well, it's primarily used by farmers as a kind of fertilizer, but … Have you ever heard of the Oklahoma City Bombing, April 11, 1995?"

"I wasn't even a year old then." Lisa shook her head.

"Yeah, me, too. Anyway, a couple of guys in a truck blew up an entire government building in Oklahoma City, killed over a hundred and fifty people."

"Oh wow! How awful!"

"Yeah, and they did it with a truckload of, you guessed it, ammonium nitrate."

"Oh my god! So that stuff is explosive?"

"Yup. I really don't know anything about how one goes about detonating it, but putting a load of it into a reaction and then heating it up doesn't sound to me like a smart thing to do."

"Wow." Lisa sat back under the weight of realizing what this all meant. "It's hard to imagine that Jodi would put that into her reaction by accident, but…" She pondered this and then said slowly, "So, if somebody, meaning Rathburn, told her to put that in there… what was his intention?"

Mariah and Lisa looked at each other, letting the question and obvious answer hang.

Mariah broke the silence. "Listen, I've got to go right now. My parents are waiting. We can talk some more about this tomorrow, okay?"

"Yeah, okay," responded Lisa as if in a daze, still contemplating the magnitude of what she had just been told.

"Alright, see ya later," Mariah called as she headed for the door.

Lisa sat and stared at nothing in the center of the room. "Had Jodi put ammonium nitrate into her reaction accidentally instead of sodium acetate?" she wondered. "Or had Rathburn told her to put the ammonium nitrate in? Would Rathburn really try to cause Jodi harm?" It seemed incredible to imagine. But what was she going to do? Lisa looked back at her desk and the list of tasks that she had only just begun ticking off. "How can I possibly concentrate on any of these now with what I have just learned? I've got to call Andy." She picked up her phone and started to punch Andy's number, but then stopped. "Oh crud! He's probably in the middle of some interview." She cancelled the call. "What was it that Officer Jenkins had said? Talk to the Burlington Campus Police first. Okay. I guess it's time to do that."

Lisa closed her books and stacked them on her desk. She pushed her backpack under her desk, grabbed her cellphone, donned her hat and coat, and headed for the door.

The Campus Safety Office was in a low building at the south end of campus. The building adjoined the campus mechanical shops that serviced the University-owned vehicles and other maintenance equipment such as mowers and snowblowers. Lisa silenced her phone as she trekked south across campus toward the Campus Safety Office, not wanting it to disturb her when she was meeting with the Campus Safety personnel. The door to the office was unlocked, but the lights were off and there was no receptionist. Still, she could see a light shining from the doorway of an office near the back, so she rang the bell on the receptionist's counter. The creak of a chair from the back office let her know that she had been heard, and a dark form lumbered down the hallway toward her. As he entered the lobby where she stood, Lisa recognized the face of Steven Davis, the Campus Safety Officer. His impatience at being interrupted was evident. "Yes?" he asked gruffly.

Lisa doubled her resolve and spoke. "I believe that we, uh I, have evidence that a crime has been committed, or is being committed, on this campus." She thought that her words must sound odd, even to her own ears, but she went on. "I'm here because I think that I should report this to somebody in authority."

Davis took this in without showing any reaction, and then looked around behind her. "Is there anybody else here with you?"

"No. Just me," replied Lisa.

"Hmmm, well, come on back here and we'll fill out a report."

Davis turned and lumbered back down the darkened hallway to his office.

The room was small and smelled of old French fries. He plopped himself down in a chair that creaked under his weight. His desk was stacked with papers and notebooks. Three filing cabinets were likewise covered with a hodge-podge of three-ring binders. Davis offered Lisa a chair adjacent to his desk and pulled a yellow-colored form from one of his drawers. Finally locating a pen, he began asking her questions and jotting down her answers on the form. Lisa recounted her evidence as succinctly as she could present it, the explosion, their analysis, and the conclusion that Ecstasy was being made, and that someone had put ammonium nitrate into Jodi's reaction flask. Feeling a touch of pride at her and Andy's achievement, she looked up to see what Davis would say when she finished.

Davis was looking at her coldly. "You weren't supposed to go in there. That area was all taped off and supposed to remain untouched until the state inspectors got there."

Somewhat taken aback that she wasn't being praised for their work, she said, "Well, we thought that we could help if we could figure out what went wrong."

"Messing with the evidence could get you into a lot of trouble," he added.

Lisa looked down at her hands. "Yeah, I guess," she admitted.

Davis sat and regarded Lisa for a long moment as if trying to decide what to do. Then, in what appeared to be a new wave of friendliness, he said, "Well. What's done is done, I guess. That's quite a story. Okay. So, I'm going to have to do some investigating and we'll see what comes up. Alright? And for now, little lady, I suggest that you go back to your studies and try to keep your nose out of trouble. Okay?" He looked her in the eye and waited.

Feeling as if she were being completely patronized and written off, Lisa regarded Davis sourly. Reluctantly she got up, collected her things, and returned to the science building. Several words came to her lips that she would have been disciplined for using as a child.

Chapter 21   2016, April 17, Sunday

Jamie dropped Andy off in front of his apartment on the corner of 18th and Tower shortly before noon. He opened the outer door and went up the stairs to the second floor. His roommate was not at home. After dumping his duffel in his room and grabbing a Coke from the fridge, he flopped on the couch and thought about Lisa and how unsettling it was when he couldn't communicate with her. "Am I that dependent on her that I can't get through twenty-four hours without talking to her?" he wondered. He felt a little ashamed that the answer to his question was probably "yes". And then his phone rang.

"Lisa! Hey, it's good to hear from you. Where have you been?"

"Andy, hey, I'm sorry. I put my phone on silent yesterday and forgot to take it off. Sorry I missed all those texts from you. Do you want to go to the library? We need to talk."

Relief flooded in at hearing her voice. "Yeah, that would be great. I'll come by your place in fifteen minutes." There was plenty of studying to be done before Monday and doing it in the company of Lisa gave him all the motivation he needed to get focused and get going. He sorted his books and notebooks into his backpack, threw on his coat and went out. Fifteen minutes later he was standing on the sidewalk as Lisa came out onto her porch.

"Hey-ya," he greeted her as she came down the steps.

"Hey," she looked up at him and smiled. They turned and walked side-by-side toward campus.

"So how was the job fair?" she asked.

"It was really pretty good," he replied. "There were at least a couple of businesses that seemed fairly encouraging, but I was most interested in this one position working as a technician for a prof at the U of M. It wouldn't be far from where you're gonna be."

"Oh, that would be nice," agreed Lisa.

Andy continued to tell her about the fair, the successes of their classmates, and the evening at Jamie's home.

"So, what did you do?" Andy asked.

"Oh, yeah!" she said with enthusiasm remembering the information she'd gotten from Mariah and her encounter with Davis. She related to Andy what Mariah had told her about the inorganic material in Jodi's reaction. "So, for some reason, Jodi put ammonium nitrate into her reaction mixture. I just can't believe that anybody would make such a mistake by accident. So then, that means that Rathburn told her to do that. That must be what Jodi wanted to ask me about."

"Unbelievable! But Rathburn would've known what that could do, wouldn't he? That isn't just some alternate modification of the reaction conditions, is it?"

"I don't see how it could be. A mild base is needed for that reaction and ammonium nitrate just doesn't qualify." Lisa shook her head in wonder. "I can't imagine how he could think that."

"But if he knew what it could do…" continued Andy, "then why would he do that to Jodi?"

"It doesn't make sense, does it?" answered Lisa.

"Well, you're right. This should be reported."

"So that's what I did." Lisa described her visit to Steven Davis in the Campus Safety Office.

"He just put me off. He wrote my name on some form and took about six words of notes and told me to go back to my studies and stay out of trouble. I can't believe that he isn't taking this more seriously."

They walked on in silence for a few minutes.

"Well, maybe he has to do some more checking or something," she said with a shake of her head. "Even so, he doesn't have to act like such a creep. He seems so patronizing. Like 'What do you know, little girl?' and 'Go run along and go back to school.'"

"Well, he's got your report. He can't just ignore that. Maybe he really will start an investigation," Andy offered hopefully. "I wonder how we'll know if he does find anything?"

"Yeah. I wonder," she replied as they crossed 21st St. onto the Burlington Campus. "I guess we'll just have to wait until we hear from him or someone else." The grandeur of the library greeted them and pushed away the thoughts of Davis and the trouble resulting from Jodi's explosion. The quiet of the great hall was calming. Their favorite table was vacant, and they settled down across from each other under the glow from a green glass-shaded lamp.

Two hours later, Andy rose and motioned to Lisa that he was headed to the lobby for a break. She, likewise, set down her pen and accompanied him out of the room. In the outer room Lisa spoke up, "Hey, would you like to go drop in on Jodi later? See how she's doing?"

"Yeah. We could do that. Shall we go about five o'clock, and then we can grab some food afterwards?"

"Sounds good."

Later that afternoon, they retrieved Andy's car and again made the trip south to Memorial Hospital. They went straight to the fifth floor. As they came to the door to what had been Jodi's room, they saw that it was open and the lights inside were off. They could see that the room was vacant. The bed had been remade, and it looked like it was all prepared for a new occupant. With a twinge of bewilderment, they first looked up and down the hallway, and then Andy pointed toward the lighted nurse's station a little farther down the hall. He approached the counter and asked the nurse, "Ah, we're friends of Jodi Sanders who used to be in room 512. And that room seems to be empty now. Can you tell us where she's gone?"

The nurse looked up at him and made a wry face. "Sorry, I'm really not supposed to say anything. Privacy rules, you know. But registration down on second might be able to tell you something."

Lisa and Andy exchanged puzzled looks. "But…" Andy began, "is she…"

"Don't worry," volunteered the nurse, "I think you'll find it's good news."

"Maybe she's gone home," said Lisa. "That would be good news."

"Thanks," said Andy as they turned and retreated to the elevator.

Riding down Lisa said, "I really would like to talk to her. Do you think that if she's gone home that her memory is better? I wonder if we can go see her. Where is her home, anyway?"

"I'm not sure, but I bet Jamie knows. I'll give him a call." Standing outside in the growing dusk, Andy punched in Jamie's number. In a moment, he was back. "Her home is in Cloquet. About twenty minutes away. He gave me her number," he said punching his cellphone.

A woman's voice came on that Andy thought he recognized as Mrs. Sanders. "Ah, hello. This is Andy Treydon. I'm a friend of Jodi's. Yeah. You may remember that we stopped in to see her a couple of times in the hospital. Yeah, right. Uh-huh. Um, say, would it be okay if Lisa and I were to stop by. Yeah, tonight." There was a pause while Andy could hear muffled voices in the background. Then, "No, we wouldn't stay long. Yeah. Sure thing. Okay. We'll be there in about half an hour. Yeah. We've got the address. Okay. Bye."

Andy turned to Lisa. "It's all good. She'd love to see us."

"Great. Let's go."

Andy punched Jodi's address into the map app on his phone and they were on their way. Traveling north on Tower Avenue led them directly onto I-535 and then onto I-35 just as they had gone to the job fair. Except that this time just a few miles down the highway they got off at the Cloquet exit. After navigating a few city streets, Andy pulled up in front of the Sanders' residence, a small white clapboard bungalow. The house and yard were neatly kept, with a row of manicured shrubs bordering a porch that extended across the front of the house. In warmer weather, the south-facing porch would be a pleasant place to sit and enjoy a cool summer evening, but now the winter storm windows were on, and several snow shovels were stacked next to the door.

Andy rang the doorbell and they were promptly greeted by Mrs. Sanders who they recognized from their several visits to the hospital. "Come in, come in," she welcomed them enthusiastically. "How nice to see you again." They entered the small entryway and shed their coats. A small living room to their left featured a fireplace that had a fire burning merrily. This was flanked on either side by bookshelves. A couch, several overstuffed chairs, reading lamps and occasional tables made a totally attractive and inviting scene. Straight ahead were stairs that led up, and to their right, through a wide arched doorway was a dining room. Behind this was a doorway that presumably led to a kitchen from which Jodi emerged looking wide awake and eager.

"Andy! Lisa! Thanks for coming." Jodi walked briskly into the room, came over to them and hugged each of them in turn.

"Jodi, you look great. How are you?" Lisa asked.

"Set your coats down, come on in, have a seat." Jodi motioned to the chairs in the living room. "I'm feeling pretty good, really. Everything is coming back."

"Wow. That is good news," said Andy.

"Do you think that you might come back to school yet this spring?" asked Lisa. "Or will you be taking the rest of the semester off?"

"Well, the doctors told me to be cautious and take it easy, but I'm definitely thinking that I'll be back to classes this week," Jodi replied.

"Wow. That's great." enthused Lisa.

"I bet they'd let you have an extension if you wanted one," suggested Andy.

"Yeah, I know that's an option. The doctors said that if I get headaches or start feeling bad that I should ease up, but actually I've been feeling better every day. And I really don't want to miss any more school. Finals are only three weeks away and I'd really like to finish the semester."

"That would be great if you're up to it. We'd love to see you back."

"Thanks. I just figure that I won't have missed that much if I get right back in now. I'm afraid that it will be a lot harder to finish up if I put things off."

"What about your lab project with Rathburn?" Lisa asked cautiously. "How are you feeling about that?"

Jodi looked down at her hands in her lap as a wave of seriousness came over her. "I don't think that I'll be going back to that. He can fail me if he wants or give me an incomplete. But I won't be working for him anymore."

"But you've put in almost two semesters of work with him," said Andy. "What will you do about the requirement for research credit?"

Jodi thought briefly. "I've got another year before graduation. If Rathburn doesn't let me have credit for what I've already done, I'll work for Barton or Martinelli."

Andy and Lisa nodded their agreement. After a pause, Lisa asked, "Jodi, would you mind if I asked you about what you were doing for Rathburn?"

"Yeah, I guess," she replied. "He told me that I wasn't supposed to talk about it with anybody, but I'm thinking that perhaps I should tell you guys, or somebody." She looked down at her hands gripped tightly in her lap.

"Well, we've also been doing a bit of detective work since you've been away, so we have some idea of what you were working on," said Andy. "But we'd like to hear your side of the story."

Lisa told her about their efforts to analyze the components of her reaction that exploded, and their conclusions. Finally she asked, "So, did you know that Rathburn was having you make illegal drugs for him?"

Jodi continued to study her hands. "No, not really. But it doesn't surprise me now. I was just running the reactions that he told me to. He would take the products that I made, and then give me a different reaction to run. I didn't know where the products were going. He said they were intermediates that he would send to SynZac."

"Yeah," said Andy, "the reaction you were doing when the explosion occurred was designed to create a precursor for the drug Ecstasy. Except, he told you to put ammonium nitrate in there, and that's why it exploded."

Jodi looked up, wide-eyed, a look of recognition on her face. "That's right!" she exclaimed, "Now I remember. Ammonium nitrate. I thought that was weird. Remember, Lisa? I called you over to look at my notebook. I'd run reactions like that before, but never with ammonium nitrate."

"So, what we don't get," said Andy, "is why he told you to do that. Do you think he knew that you would have an explosion?"

Jodi's face fell again. "Having me make a precursor for Ecstasy is not so surprising now." She became hesitant. "He…he… came on to me. It was while we were planning the reaction in his office. He tried to kiss me. He was putting his hands on me. Then he told me that he could get me drugs, well, Ecstasy, and others, I guess. And that we should take it together and then have sex. I couldn't believe it. It was so awful."

"Oh, my god," said Lisa, holding her hands to her face.

"I told him 'No'," Jodi went on. "I told him I didn't want him to touch me. I told him that I didn't want to have anything to do with his drugs. I got to the door, but then he called me back and told me to change the reaction ingredients. That's when he said to put the ammonium nitrate in there instead of what we had been using. It wasn't unusual for him to make modifications to the reaction conditions, so I didn't think too much about it until I got back to the lab."

"Oh, Jodi. I'm so sorry that you had to go through that." Lisa reached out and put her hand on Jodi's arm.

"You should know, we've gone to the police," Andy added. "And Lisa has told the Campus Safety Officer, Mr. Davis. But as far as we know they haven't done anything yet."

"But maybe we should go see them again, now that we've talked to you," said Lisa.

"I don't know," said Jodi shaking her head slowly. She rubbed her forehead. "I still have moments when I'm not sure if I remember things correctly."

"Well, we aren't going to pressure you. You don't have to do anything until you're ready. But what you have told us tonight confirms a lot of our suspicions. I think that dirt-bag Rathburn has really gone over the line, and somebody should take him down," Andy stated emphatically.

The room was quiet for a while, only the crackling of the fire in the hearth could be heard. Then Lisa arose and went over and stood by Jodi with her hand on her shoulder. "I'm just glad that you are okay, Jodi. That's the most important thing."

"Thanks, Lisa. Thanks, Andy. You guys are great."

Lisa and Andy put on their coats and headed for the door. "Well, we've gotta be going. I hope we didn't upset you," said Lisa.

"No, no," Jodi replied. "It's all been running around up here in a jumble anyway," she said pointing to her head and twirling her finger.

"Well, let us know when you're coming back. Maybe we'll bake you a cake or something." Andy smiled and touched Jodi's hand.

"Well, it's gotta be pretty soon. I've got to get back at it if I want to finish the semester, and I've got to get back and keep Abby company," Jodi mused.

Lisa paused, "Why's that?"

"My roommate, Abby Decker, I called her yesterday to let her know what's going on. You knew that she was going with our other roommate, Jordan Lewis, didn't you? Well, they just broke up and he moved out. So, she's kinda having a hard time. I think it would help her if she weren't all alone in our house right now."

"Really? Abby and Jordan? They've been a thing for quite a long time, haven't they?"

"Yeah. They were. I don't really know what happened, but Abby's pretty broken up about it."

"Well, good luck. And let us know if you need any help moving back," added Andy. "It'll be great to see you around the department."

They waved goodbye and walked out to Andy's car. Riding back to Superior they were silent for a while. Finally Andy commented, "That Rathburn is such a dirtbag."

"That man is evil and something needs to be done," said Lisa.

Chapter 22   2016, April 17, Sunday

Cynthia awoke to the sound of Rathburn's voice coming from the next room. She got out of bed, grabbed a robe, and started toward the bathroom, but paused by the half-open door. Charles was taking on his phone, but the stress in his voice was unmistakable. "No. I don't see any reason that I need to meet with them. No. You can talk to them for me." Then in a more defeated tone he said, "Okay, okay, I'll be there. Just, just…. Oh fuck it!" He ended the call.

Cynthia hurried into the bathroom so that she wouldn't be discovered eavesdropping. She pivoted, flushed the toilet and was just stepping into the bedroom when Charles came in from the outer room. "Good morning, Charles," she greeted him brightly.

"Oh, heck," he growled. "I've got to go and meet with some business associates. I don't believe it. Sunday morning. You'd think they could at least pretend to be civilized."

Cynthia had seen Rathburn in grumpy moods before and knew that there would be no cajoling or mollifying. The best course for her would be to stand aside and let him grump his way along until it played out. Then he'd realize what a fool he had been and pretend that it had never happened. Eventually the sweet-talking gentleman would re-emerge, and life would be rosy until the next event happened that he could interpret as a specifically targeted offense to his sense of self-importance.

Cynthia made a beeline for the coffee pot in the kitchen while Rathburn threw on his clothes and prepared to leave. Wandering into the spacious carpeted living room in her bathrobe, bare feet and carrying a steaming mug she watched Rathburn angrily gather some papers into his briefcase, look in the mirror, adjust his tie, don his camel-hair coat and open the door to their apartment. He paused and looked back at Cynthia. "I'm not sure when I'll be back, so don't expect me."

"Okay, Charles," she said lightly, smiling faintly.

He went out and closed the door behind him.

A short drive across town brought Rathburn to the large, corrugated metal-sided warehouse that occupied nearly a city block directly west across Banks Street from the Sea Shanty Saloon. Large red letters that spelled out "KAM" adorned one side of the building facing the street with the explanatory "Koreo Amerain Mercantile" in smaller letters below. At the north end, a gravel driveway led up to two oversized roll-up doors, with a standard human-sized service door to one side. Charles parked his car next to the service door and entered without knocking.

The interior was dimly lit by occasional overhead lights dangling from the high ceiling. In one corner an office room had been sectioned off from the rest of the large floor with walls that had windows comprising the upper half. On one wall adjacent to the office was a large sink with water faucets, a collection of mops, buckets and brooms, and a door that presumably led to a bathroom or closet. An old pickup truck and two fork-lifts were parked just inside the large overhead doors. Toward the rear of this space, a dividing wall separated this outer area from a larger storage space at the south end of the building. A couple of overhead doors in this wall allowed the fork-lifts to move their pallets of goods from the loading area back to longer term storage. Rathburn walked directly to this back wall and through a service door into the main storage area. Here, pallets of goods were stacked in long rows all the way to the far end of the building. But just inside the wall was a second office with half windowed walls. The lights were glowing inside, and Rathburn could see the familiar face of Steven Davis together with a large man, Dugan Jones, whom he had met on a couple of previous, rather unpleasant, occasions. "Oh, great," he thought, "he's brought the intelligentsia." Rathburn stepped into the doorway of the office.

"Hello Steven. Hello Dugan," he greeted them civilly.

"Good. He's here," Dugan grunted. Dugan, who looked like his main occupation in life might be that of a night club bouncer, leaned against the back wall with his muscular arms folded across his chest.

"We've got a problem," Davis began. "Or rather you've got a problem," he said pointing at Rathburn.

"Why is that?" asked Charles.

"The students that you have involved in this little project are starting to leak information."

"What? How?" Rathburn tried to appear innocent.

"I'll tell you how," replied Davis, rising from his chair. "That first one is out of the hospital. All recovered it seems. Now who knows what she is going to say, or has already said to who."

"To whom," Rathburn thought as he looked at the floor and shook his head faintly.

"And now there is this one." Davis held up a yellow-colored paper and waved it. "It seems that this young lady has gone and figured it all out!" He looked at the form in his hand. "She's deduced that you're making Ecstasy, and that you put something," he looked at the sheet, "ammonia something, whatever, in the first girl's reaction to make it explode. I think it looks like your involvement in this is getting to be a big liability."

Rathburn pursed his lips and tried to think of something to say. "Look. These students are going to graduate soon. They will go away. Maybe if we just cool it for a while, this will all blow over." He looked from one to the other.

"It may already be too late," said Davis. "This second student," he looked at his yellow form, "a Lisa Ross, has already gone to the police."

"What," said Rathburn, looking up. "Lisa Ross? How? The Police?"

"Yeah. I got a call from Superior PD, telling me that she had been there. They aren't going to come onto campus until I ask them to, but they are hanging out there watching."

"Oh, shit," said Rathburn. Suddenly the room started to feel warm, and a couple of beads of perspiration formed on his brow. "Well, okay, I see that we've got to do something." Rathburn felt his legs weakening underneath him, and he moved to sit in one of the unoccupied chairs in the office, but Dugan stepped forward and grasped the lapels of Rathburn's coat.

"Hey, hey, don't…" Rathburn protested watching Dugan's unwashed hands on his light-colored coat.

"Don't nothing," said Dugan. "You've got one week to fix this. Or less. You figure out some way to get rid of these students, or shut them up permanently, or we are going to do it for you. But if we do it, then you are going along with them. Understand? That's a mighty big lake out there and it's a long way to the bottom, if you know what I mean?"

Rathburn stared wide-eyed at Dugan. He thought of protesting but stopped himself.

"Just to make sure that you don't forget," said Dugan loosening his grip, "we have a little goodbye present for you."

Dugan pushed Rathburn through the door and followed him onto the warehouse floor. "Okay, Mr. Fancy-pants," he hissed. Faster that Rathburn could see it coming, Dugan swung his fist deep into Rathburn's belly. Charles doubled over and fell to the floor retching. "Come on, you pussy," he said, and grabbed Rathburn's coat and lifted him back to a standing position. When Charles was almost upright, Dugan punched him again squarely on his nose. Again, Charles was on the floor, holding his bleeding face. Dugan looked down at him and then back at Davis. "More?"

Davis shook his head, "No, I think he's got the message."

Dugan delivered a hard kick to Rathburn's ribs and walked back into the office. Davis stood over Rathburn. "You better get out of here while you can still walk, Charley."

Holding his hand over his nose, Rathburn got onto his knees and then stumbled to his feet. Half running, he fled out the door from which he had entered. At his car, he fetched a rag from his trunk and tried to wipe up the blood on his face and his clothes. His fine coat was a mess. The grease from rolling around on the floor and his own blood made it a total disaster. He threw it into the trunk of his car and checked himself over before deciding whether he could get in without dirtying his upholstery. Looking up and seeing Davis coming out the service door made up his mind for him. He jumped in and sped out of the parking lot with a spray of gravel.

⚗

Later that evening Cynthia heard Charles come in the door of the apartment. Looking up from her studying spread out on the high kitchen counter to one side of the living room, she was appalled at his appearance. "Charles! What happened? Look at you!"

Rathburn threw his soiled coat into a pile on the foyer tile and walked over to the bar. Cynthia came up to him, trying to examine his damaged face. "Charles! What happened to you?"

"I got mugged," he growled.

"Mugged?" Cynthia replied, "In Superior?"

"Yeah," was his curt reply. Cynthia waited.

Recognizing that his explanation was insufficient he went on, "Yeah, I stopped for a beer at the Sea Shanty and when I came out there were a couple of guys…" he waved his hand in the air and waited to see whether Cynthia would accept this.

"Did you call the police?"

"No, no. They ran off. It was dark. I would never be able to identify them."

"But did they rob you?" she asked.

"No," he replied. He reached inside the breast pocket of his jacket and fingered his wallet. "I just think that I may have offended them somehow inside, and they just hit me a couple of times outside. That was it." He looked at her, hoping that he wouldn't have to say more.

Cynthia was sure that she was being told a fairytale but decided that if Rathburn wasn't going to tell her more, then she wasn't going to win any points by trying to wheedle more out of him. "Here, let me clean you up," she said, trying to sound motherly. Cynthia grabbed a couple of tissues, wetted one, and started dabbing at Charles' face. He took her ministrations for a few minutes and then pushed her away.

"I'm not going to stay tonight," he announced. "I'm going to go home. I'll see you tomorrow, I guess."

"Okay, Charles. Whatever you say," Cynthia agreed. She watched Rathburn go to the door and scoop up his soiled coat. Pausing, he turned back to look at her. Then he came back to where she was standing and gave her a quick peck. "Thanks for being here," he said. "Take care." Cynthia put her arms around him and attempted to give him a hug, but he recoiled and pushed her off. "Ow, ow. Don't do that," he said putting a hand up to protect his injured ribs. At Cynthia's look of concern, he shook his head and said, "Don't ask." He went out the door and closed it behind him.

Cynthia watched as he left and stood looking at the backside of the door. She thought about what Rathburn had told her and the phone call that he had taken earlier. And then she thought about her mother's advice. "I don't think that was just a random mugging," she mused. She went to the bedroom, removed a suitcase from the closet and began packing her clothes. "Yep, I'm afraid it's time for our association to end, Charley, dear."

Chapter 23**2016, April 18, Monday**

Curled up under the warmth of his blankets, Andy slowly drifted into consciousness. His first thoughts were of Lisa. He savored the image of her face smiling at him, her gently curled light brown ponytail that bounced as she moved, and the boundless energy that seemed to simmer beneath her driven personality. "What a girl, well, woman, well yes, whatever," he thought. "I want her, whoever she is. I want to be with her." But then the gnawing question intruded, "But does she want me?"

"Enough!" he thought, as he threw off his covers, bounded out of bed and got dressed. After a quick Pop-Tart and a glass of milk, he shouldered his backpack and set off for campus. Buoyed by an unknown source of energy, the walk to campus seemed to fly by. Andy took the stairs two at a time to the third floor of the science building and strode the hallway toward the student assistants' lounge. As he passed the departmental office, he encountered Dr. Barton coming out the door.

"Hey, Andy! Come with me. I've got to find something in Dr. Rathburn's office. Maybe you can help."

"Okay," Andy replied. He did an about face and followed Dr. Barton back the way he had come to Rathburn's office. Dr. Barton pulled a key from his pocket and opened the door.

"This is not what I need right now," Dr. Barton muttered half to himself and half to Andy. "I got a call from Rathburn last night at eleven o'clock. Eleven o'clock! Got me out of bed. Turns out he's sick. 'Sick' he says. Would you believe it? Right! Very probably he won't be coming back to school for three or four days he says. Good grief! And now it's up to me to figure out how we're going to cover all of his classes between now and whenever he deigns to grace us with his presence again." Barton had switched on the light and was starting to poke into some of the stacks of papers on Rathburn's desk. Pausing momentarily, he turned to Andy. "Okay. He has four classes. Hopefully we should be able to find at least a file folder for each one. His syllabi are on file, but it'd be good if we could find his topic schedule or his lecture notes, something to indicate where to pick up. The files should have labels for an organic lecture, a gen chem lecture, an organic lab and a gen chem lab. Until I get his password, I doubt there's any point in looking at his computer. So, you look over there in that pile and I'll look here." They busied themselves examining the stacks of papers and notebooks.

"I think I found the student notebooks for his organic lab," said Andy as he recognized a stack of notebooks that were typical of the type that students used in that course. He flipped the first one open to examine the list of experiments to see whether they were the ones that he knew were commonly used in that course. He gathered up the stack, preparing to transport it out of Rathburn's office when he noticed one in the middle of the stack that had a different style of binding than the others. Andy pulled it out. The frontispiece read, "Research, 2015-2016, J. Sanders". Jodi's Notebook! "Aha, this is it!" he exclaimed, and then looked up to see whether his outburst had been noticed. Barton remained busily looking in a pile of papers with his back turned. Quickly Andy slid Jodi's notebook into his backpack and returned to straighten the pile of student notebooks.

When Barton was satisfied that they had found enough, Andy helped him carry a stack of papers and files back to his office. "I'll get Martinelli to finish up the lecture course, and I can do Rathburn's lab…" he was muttering. "Let's see, I'll have to talk to Miller about whether he can do the gen chem lab, or…" he trailed off. "Okay, just set those there," he said to Andy. "Thanks for the help. I can take it from here." Andy resumed his journey to the student assistants' lounge where he met Gary and Kayla coming out the door. "See you in class," Kayla chirped merrily as they passed. Andy could hardly contain his eagerness to tell Lisa what he had found. He dumped his coat and backpack at his desk, grabbed his notebook and sped across the hall to Dr. Martinelli's eight o'clock advanced organic class. Lisa was already seated, and he slipped into the chair next to hers. He leaned over and whispered, "I found it! Jodi's notebook."

Lisa looked at him wide-eyed. "Oh my God! Where? How did you get it?"

"Barton asked me to help him look for some stuff in Rathburn's office. It was in there among the notebooks for his organic lab. I've got it in my backpack."

"Andy! That's fantastic. Ooh, I want to see it."

Dr. Martinelli cleared her throat and looked over the top of her glasses at Andy and Lisa, who straightened up and turned their attention to the front of the room.

When class was over, Lisa and Andy rushed back to the student assistants' lounge. "Let me see it," urged Lisa. Andy pulled it out of his backpack and handed it to Lisa who turned it over and read the identification on its front. The surface showed a couple of stains, now dried, that had likely been incurred on the day of the explosion. They paged through the notebook and noted that several of the reactions that had been recorded did specifically describe the conversion of an intermediate into the chemical compound, Ecstasy. Turning to the last entry, they examined the list of ingredients. Sure enough, the reactants were indeed the exact chemicals that they had deduced from their analyses of the materials that they had recovered from her fume hood. And, the inorganic component was, as Mariah had deduced, ammonium nitrate. Andy nodded and looked at Lisa. "We got it right, didn't we?"

"We sure did," she replied. They smiled at each other and executed a high five. Then, more seriously, Lisa continued. "It seems then, that together with what Jodi told us, it's pretty clear that Rathburn intentionally instructed Jodi to put the ammonium nitrate in there. I think this is pretty damning."

"So, now I guess we wait and see what Davis is going to do, huh? Or do we go show it to him as further proof?" asked Andy.

"I don't know. Let's think about it," replied Lisa. "But right now, I've got to think about a Dif EQ test that is coming up in an hour. So where are we going to keep this?"

"How about right here," Andy suggested, pulling open one of his desk drawers.

"Fine," responded Lisa. She went to her desk and picked up a text and a notebook. "I'm going over to Donley Hall. I can study in my classroom there until it's test time. I'll see you later." She grabbed her coat and walked out of the room.

Andy turned back to his desk but not until he looked around to see who else was present in the room. Kayla was at her desk on the far side, apparently trying to study while Gary sat nearby apparently trying to study Kayla. Cynthia was sitting closer to him, and she had swiveled her chair around so that she was facing him. Andy realized that it had been totally possible that Cynthia could have overheard his and Lisa's entire conversation. Their eyes met and Cynthia moved her chair closer. In a soft voice she said, "Charley Rathburn has been up to no good, has he?"

Andy hesitated, knowing that Cynthia worked for Rathburn and consulted with him regularly. He wasn't sure how much of what he told her might get back to Rathburn. But then he decided that there was no real need for secrecy. "Yeah. I think he's in real trouble, and something's going to happen."

"Yeah, what kind of trouble?"

"Well," Andy began, trying to think about how confident he was of the evidence that he and Lisa had found, "for one, we're pretty sure that he was having Jodi make Ecstasy in the lab." He paused, wondering whether Cynthia might also have been doing this too, and that she already knew about this. He shot her a hard look but could see no recognition in her expression. Plowing ahead he added, "And two, we think that he told Jodi to add something to her last reaction that was the cause of her explosion. Like he was trying to harm her, or even kill her."

"Holy shit!" said Cynthia covering her mouth with her hand. She looked at the floor and shook her head slowly from side to side. Then with a change of thought, she started nodding in what seemed like sad acceptance. "I bet you're right, I bet you're right." Then, she asked, "So what are you going to do?"

"Well, we've already gone to the police, but they said to talk to campus security. So, Lisa has been there, but so far we can't tell that they are doing anything."

"Hmmm," responded Cynthia thinking this over. Then, changing the topic, she said, "Hey, Andy, it turns out that I have to relocate on rather short notice. Do you know anybody who has an unoccupied room or even a couch I could crash on until the end of the semester?"

Initially puzzled by this somewhat surprising piece of information, Andy started to shake his head, 'no', but then stopped. "Wait. Actually, I might. Jodi Sanders is coming back to campus. I heard that one of her roommates has just moved out. I bet you could move in there. Even for one month, I bet they'd be glad to get the help with the rent."

"With Jodi? She's back?"

"Yeah. I saw her last night. She's looking really good. She's hoping to finish all her classes this semester."

"Wow. Good news. Jodi and I have always gotten along well. Moving in with her would be great," said Cynthia. "Do you know who her roommate is?"

"Yeah, I think its Abbey Decker. It was Jordan Lewis who moved out."

Cynthia nodded. "Just as well. I never liked Jordan. Anyway, could you contact them and see if it would be possible?"

"Yeah, I can do that. Um, I'm going to have to find some numbers to call, so hang on a sec, okay?" Andy started to scroll through the contact list on his phone.

Cynthia watched him for a minute and then moved closer. "Andy," she began, "do you remember that night a long time ago, on the balcony of the UC, our freshman week?"

"I sure do," replied Andy pausing his search through his phone.

"I wish that we had ah… pursued things more, you know? You're a good guy. I'm sorry that, well, you know… that we let it get away." She looked at him wistfully.

Andy squelched his feelings of surprise. "I don't know why we didn't stick together after that, Cyn, but I guess it is just the way things work out sometimes." Andy did feel some pangs of regret. He had been attracted to Cynthia and still harbored some feelings that way. But Cynthia had spent the intervening years acting distant and aloof. This had built a wall that wasn't going to come down with one declaration of regret. But, more importantly, his current involvement with Lisa didn't allow him any room to consider thoughts of any kind of relationship with Cynthia. It was just out of the question.

Shaking off the thoughts that she had provoked, he went back to searching his phone for Jodi's number. After a short conversation, and then a second call to Abby, Andy turned back to Cynthia. "It's all arranged. I don't believe how easy that was. Here's the code for the entry lock. They both would be glad to have you move in. Their lease is up in August, so you can stay as long as you want, even take over their lease for next year, if you want. Jodi will be here for another year. Not sure about Abby."

"I won't be staying longer than a month," said Cynthia. "Crane Analytical will take me on as soon as I can get to Racine, so when finals are over, I'm outta here."

"Really? How about graduation?"

"I'm not going to stay for it. I've got nobody to come and watch me walk."

"I'm sorry to hear that, Cyn. I guess that I never realized how much you are on your own."

"Well, I guess I'm pretty independent," she said proudly. "I like it that way." But the latter statement sounded unconvincing. Andy regarded her, wondering how much of Cynthia's brave exterior was just for show.

He turned back to his desk, but Cynthia persisted. "Ah, Andy, sorry to ask you one more thing, but could you help me move my stuff? It won't take long, it isn't a lot, but some of it's kind of awkward. Could you help me? Please?"

Andy looked around, beginning to feel a little exasperated at the number of unforeseen requests for his time. "Well, okay, I guess. When do you want to do this?"

"Right now. Or this afternoon. As soon as possible."

"Wow. This relocation really came up fast, didn't it?"

"Yeah, yeah…" she said mysteriously. "I'll tell you about it later."

Andy looked at his desk and considered his schedule for the day. "Well, I've got an eleven o'clock class, and then I'm assisting in a gen chem lab from two until five, so I guess that we can do this over the noon hour, if you think that will be enough time.

"Should be more than enough," said Cynthia. "I'll meet you in front of my apartment at noon; here's the address." She handed him a slip of paper and put her hand on Andy's and smiled at him.

"Oh Jeez. What the heck am I getting into?" thought Andy.

Shortly before noon Andy left the science building, fetched his car and made the short drive to Cynthia's apartment. As he pulled up in front, Andy marveled at the fancy exterior of the tall building where Cynthia was waiting for him under the covered entryway. She punched a code into the box in the wall, and the door buzzed to admit them to a large foyer with lounge chairs and potted plants. They entered the elevator and rode in silence to the eighth floor. Andy was astounded when he entered the apartment. The large sunken living room with floor-to-ceiling windows with a view of Lake Superior, a huge flat-screen television, the adjacent spacious kitchen, the adjoining dining room, all furnished with quality pieces seemed like something from a movie. "My god, Cyn! This is where you've been living while you've been going to Burlington? This is fantastic!" He held out his arms and did a slow turnabout. Cynthia motioned for him to follow her as she led him into the bedroom. The bedroom was equally impressive. It was spacious with a king-sized bed, several dressers, one wall of floor-to-ceiling windows covered by gauzy white curtains, a doorway that led into a large, tiled bathroom and an equally large walk-in closet. Cynthia walked to the far side of the bed where several suitcases and a couple of partially filled cardboard moving boxes stood open. As Andy looked around the room appreciating the furnishings, Cynthia stopped on the opposite side of the bed facing him. She cocked her head and gave him a look that seemed both questioning and inviting.

Andy paused and met her look. Not entirely certain what Cynthia's meaning might be, he pointed to the boxes. "Are these what you'd like me to carry down?"

The smile faded from Cynthia's face. "Yup. Just these two, and the suitcases. There're a couple more out in the kitchen."

Andy gathered up the suitcases and boxes and moved them to the hall by the front door. Finally his curiosity got the better of him. "Cynthia, I'm sorry for being so blunt, but I just gotta ask. How have you been able to afford all this?"

Cynthia came over to him, pondering how to answer his question. Then, looking him in the eye and with a hardness in her voice, she said, "You might say that I've had a sponsor."

"A 'sponsor'?"

"Yeah, a kind of friend who's paid my way."

Andy wasn't catching on. "A 'friend', you say. Nice friend! Jeesh."

Cynthia wasn't going to let Andy get away. "Yeah. A wealthy friend. He is even somebody that you might know."

"Really?" Andy was mystified.

"Yeah. I call him 'Charles'. His last name is Rathburn."

"What? Rathburn? You mean…" he pointed generally in the direction of the Burlington campus.

Cynthia nodded. Andy stood dumbfounded while he tried to understand all that was implied by what he had just learned. "But…. but… but…" he stuttered as the gears meshed in his head.

Cynthia patted Andy's arm. "Try not to think too hard about it," she said. "But get this…" she continued more seriously. "You understand why I need to get out of here now, right? Charles is in trouble, right? I don't know if the next people to come after Charles are going to be the feds, or the goons, but either way, Cynthia Collins is not going to be here when they arrive."

They stared into one another's eyes as Cynthia's meaning became firmly understood.

"Okay. I get it," Andy finally declared. He took a deep breath and looked around the room. "Okay. Let's get these boxes loaded."

As they went back to work, Andy's phone buzzed. He recognized that it was from Lisa, but not wanting the interruption, he sent it to voicemail. Cynthia finished her packing and Andy transported the boxes down the elevator to his car and to Cynthia's that was parked in a covered basement garage. After a couple of easy trips, all of her possessions were loaded. Cynthia wrote a note and left it with her key on the table just inside the front door to the apartment. Fifteen minutes later they were across town carrying Cynthia's boxes up the steps to Jodi and Abby's rental house on Hammond Avenue. Looking around the crowded, run-down conditions of Cynthia's new accommodations, Andy couldn't help but be conscious of the stark contrast with the apartment that she had just left. Still, he felt somewhat pleased that Cynthia had decided to distance herself from Rathburn. Cynthia was unpacking a box in the new bedroom that she was going to occupy when Andy carried up the last box. "Hey, Cyn, I'm going to take off. I got that lab at two o'clock."

She came out of the bedroom and smiled at him. "Thanks, Andy. Really, you've been a good friend. Thanks." Before he could resist, she turned her face to his and kissed him. "I'll see you around."

"Okay. Uh, bye," he said, as he almost stumbled, moving toward the door.

After dropping his car at his apartment building, Andy jogged back to campus, thoughts racing in his head. "My god, am I the most clueless person on the planet?" he wondered.

That same day, a little after noon, Lisa walked into the student assistants' lounge and looked around. Kayla was at her desk studying, and, for once, Gary was leaving her alone and studying as well. "Have either of you seen Andy," Lisa asked.

"Yeah. He just left," Gary spoke up.

"Yeah, he and Cynthia left together. They had their coats on," added Kayla.

"With Cynthia!" said Lisa, looking puzzled. "Hmmph." She went to Andy's desk and took Jodi's notebook from the desk drawer. At her own desk, she paged through the notebook, looking at the diagrams of the different reactions that Jodi had performed. When she got to the last entry, she thought again about how Rathburn must have purposely instructed Jodi to include an ingredient that was going to cause an explosion. This could only have been malicious. Shaking her head in disgust, she looked up. "Hey Gary, Kayla, come look at this, would you," she called.

The two got up and walked over to Lisa's desk where she showed them the notebook and explained what Rathburn had been having Jodi prepare and how his inclusion of the last ingredient had likely been the purposeful cause of her explosion.

"My god," exclaimed Kayla, "that man is a criminal!"

"This is not right," said Gary seriously.

"You know, Andy and I have already been to the police once and the campus safety officer again, and still nothing is happening to stop him."

"Why not?" asked Kayla.

"I don't know." Lisa slumped in her chair. She thumbed the edge of Jodi's notebook and thought. "I wish Andy were here," she mused. She pulled out her phone and punched in Andy's number. No answer and sent to voicemail. "Okay," she said. "I can't wait." With renewed energy she sat up. "I'm going to try one more time. Maybe he'll believe me if he sees this." She closed Jodi's notebook and put it into her backpack. Depositing the rest of her books and notebooks on her desk, she donned her coat and backpack. "If you see Andy, tell him I went to see Mr. Davis in the Safety Office," she called to Kayla and Gary and headed out the door.

Her hike to the Campus Safety Office two days ago was fresh in her memory as she walked the tree-lined sidewalks of the Burlington campus. This time, however, Monday at midday, the campus was teeming with students on their way to their various appointments. When she arrived at the Safety Office, the reception area was dark, and nobody was behind the desk. "Ah, lunch break," she surmised. As on her previous visit, she spied a light at the end of the corridor in the office that she knew to belong to Davis. She rang the bell on the receptionist's counter, and soon Mr. Davis appeared. "You again," he said in a way that was not totally unfriendly. "Alright. Come on back." He motioned with his arm and lumbered back down the hall to his office. Lisa sat in the same chair as before while Davis went back to work consuming the remains of a fast-food hamburger that lay on a wrapper on his desk.

"Whatcha got for me this time?" he asked as he crumpled the greasy paper, tossed it toward the wastebasket, and wiped his fingers on a paper napkin.

Lisa pulled out Jodi's notebook and handed it to Davis. "This is Jodi Sander's notebook that she used on the day the explosion occurred. It confirms all of the things that I told you two days ago."

"Oh really?" He held out his hand and took the notebook from Lisa. He set it on his desk without opening it and looked at the cover. "Hmmm…" he commented, and thought for a while, drumming his fingers. Then, he got up from his desk and moved toward the door. "I just had lunch. I'm going to get something to drink. You want anything?"

"No, thank you," replied Lisa.

Davis disappeared around the corner into a break room. Lisa heard a refrigerator door open, and the sound of tabs being pulled to open two soda cans. After what seemed like a long delay, Davis came back into the room carrying a Coke can in one hand and a Diet Coke can in the other. "I don't like to drink alone," he said and chuckled at his own joke. "You look like a Diet Coke kinda girl to me, so I got you one. Here," he offered the can to Lisa.

He settled his bulk back into his chair and took a long sip from his can.

Lisa took a few cautious sips and set hers down. "Well," he said, sitting forward, "it looks like you've really got the proof, this time, doesn't it?"

"Yeah, I think we do," replied Lisa feeling somewhat wary of Davis' apparent willingness to accept the new evidence. She took a sip from her can.

"Okay," he said. "Let me write this down." He opened a couple of desk drawers before he again produced a yellow-colored form and then looked in two different locations before he seemed to be able to produce a working writing instrument. Carefully dating the top of the form, he turned to her and asked, "Tell me again your full name."

"Didn't we do this last time?" asked Lisa. "Can't we just move on with this?" Lisa could feel the exasperation rising in her. "My name doesn't matter as much as what are you doing to investigate this crime that is happening right here on the Burlington Campus. Really! What are you doing about it?"

Unperturbed, Davis sat back in his chair and regarded Lisa languidly. "These things take time. Please, be patient. Everything has to be done by the book; everything has to be documented, okay?" He turned back to his yellow form. "Now, tell me again, your full name."

"Lisa Susan Ross," Lisa replied. She reached for her Diet Coke and took several swallows. Davis wrote slowly on his form. Appearing to take a slightly more serious interest in Lisa's statements, he went back over information that she had given him previously.

"Okay, and now we've got this new evidence," he said indicating the unopened notebook lying on his desk before him. He gingerly opened the cover and started looking at the pages one by one.

"Oh, good grief," thought Lisa, "this is taking forever." She took several more swallows of her Diet Coke. Davis seemed to be moving more and more slowly and looking at her suspiciously. His voice seemed to become more and more drone-like, and the room started to hum and feel strangely warm. "Uh, what was that last question?" she asked, realizing that her attention had slipped. Davis set his pen down and leaned back and looked at her. She looked back and him and wondered why she couldn't remember what he had just said. "Goodness, I feel sleepy," she thought. "I should probably go," she said looking around for her coat. Thoughts of reporting her evidence to Davis no longer seemed important. "Oh, I've got to close my eyes for just a minute," she thought, and leaned her head back against the wall behind her chair.

Ten minutes later, Marion Atkinson, the administrative assistant for the Burlington Campus Safety Office, returned from her lunch break and came in through the front door. She hung her coat on a hook and deposited her purse under her desk. Glancing through the window that gave a view to the backside of the building, she observed several events that struck her as odd. There, by the loading dock was her boss, Steven Davis, actually working. Davis, who rarely did any manual labor himself and likewise jealously guarded his lunch hour as his private downtime, had backed one of the University's large box trucks up to the loading dock and was using a dolly to wheel a large crate onto the truck. Then he closed the doors, got into the cab, and drove away. "Well, I never!" she thought. She sat down at her desk, wiggled her mouse to wake up her computer and pulled a file from her inbox.

⚗

When Andy was released from the gen chem lab that he had been assisting that afternoon, he walked back to the student assistants' lounge and looked around. His lab had run over time, and so he was not surprised that the lounge was empty. "They've probably all gone to supper," he mused. He sat at his desk and organized his notebooks and backpack for the studies that he anticipated doing later that evening. "Oh crud!" he said out loud when he recalled a macroeconomics essay assignment that he had been postponing. "I wonder if Lisa has already gone with the others or if she plans to study in the library tonight?" he thought. He punched her number into his phone and waited. No answer. He disconnected and sent a text: "Got a econ paper to write tonight. Join me in the lib?" On Lisa's desk he noted several of her usual textbooks and notebooks in a neat stack. "Hmmm…" he thought, puzzled. "She hasn't gone home." Then he checked his desk drawer where he had stowed Jodi's notebook. It was gone. "So, she has gone somewhere with the notebook," he thought. He looked around at the empty room. "Okay. So here I am, no Lisa, no notebook, and she doesn't answer her phone. I guess I'm the one in the dark." He stood, hands on hips, wondering what to do. "Well, the heck with this. I'm going to dinner, too," he thought. Pushing aside thoughts of anything else, he grabbed his coat and his backpack, and headed to the SC.

Chapter 24   2016, April 19, Tuesday

Andy opened his eyes and focused on a small patch of peeling paint on his ceiling that was barely illuminated by the warm sunlight that filtered through his make-shift curtains. Then, with a start, he sat upright, reached for his phone on the nightstand and tapped in Lisa's number. Again, the call was sent to voicemail. "Lisa!" he shouted to the empty room. "Where the heck are you? And why don't you turn your phone on?" The previous evening had been equally frustrating. No Gary, Kayla, Jamie or anyone in the SC dining room. After dinner he had gone to the library and hoped to find Lisa at the table where they usually studied. But, no luck. Andy had tried to concentrate on his own assignments, but his nagging thoughts and repeated trips to the lobby to try calling Lisa again made progress difficult. Finally, he had given up and gone back to his apartment.

Now, a new day had dawned, and Lisa was still not answering her phone. Andy wasn't sure whether he was angry that she had forgotten and left her phone turned off, or worried that something might have happened to her. Or maybe he had somehow offended her, and she was purposefully blocking his calls. "Whatever it is," he thought, "I've got to do something!"

Andy pulled on yesterday's flannel shirt and jeans, grabbed some orange juice and a Pop-Tart, shouldered his backpack and headed out the door. He made the four-block walk to Lisa's rental house in record time and flew up the porch steps. At the door to the second-floor apartments he pressed the ancient paint-coated doorbell button. There was no distant buzzer or chime that could confirm its functional integrity. His phone told him it was 7:50 in the morning. "I don't care if I wake anybody up," he thought. After waiting a full minute he pressed the doorbell again, and then pounded on the door with his fist. After another thirty seconds, he tried again. Finally, he heard somebody coming down the stairs. The curtain parted and a face appeared behind the glass; then he heard the bolt being thrown and the door opened. Lisa's roommate, Bethany Merrill, dressed in a floppy grey sweatsuit greeted him. "Hey, Andy, do you know what time it is?" Her displeasure at being awakened was evident. "What are you doing here?"

"Hi, Bethany. I'm really sorry to bother you so early, but I have been having a lot of trouble getting through to Lisa. Is she here?"

Bethany looked over her shoulder. "Ahh… I'm not sure. Hang on a sec. I'll go check." Bethany climbed the stairs while Andy fidgeted on the porch. Soon he heard her coming back down. "No. She's not here," she said with a slight note of surprise in her voice.

"Any idea when you last saw her?" Andy queried.

"Um, let me think a sec. I guess it was the day before yesterday. Sunday. We pretty much come and go on our own, you know. And I'm not always here. So, she could have been here last night and I wouldn't have known." She paused and then added, "Come to think of it, I got here about eight last night and I didn't see her all evening. I went to bed about eleven. Unless she was already asleep in her room. But she's not there now. I just don't know."

Andy grimaced. "It's just that I've been calling and texting her since yesterday afternoon, and I've gotten zero response. I really don't think that she is trying to avoid me, but I just don't know where to turn. Do you have any idea where she might be?"

Bethany gave Andy a knowing smile. "From what I hear I don't think that she would try to avoid you. But, no, I'm sorry. I really have no idea where she might be."

"Well, thanks, Bethany. If you learn anything from anyone else or hear from her, would you please give me a call? I'm really getting worried." Andy turned and descended the porch stairs. "Sorry to have bothered you," he called. At the sidewalk he paused, looked right and left, and then with his hands in his coat pockets walked slowly toward campus.

Andy lumbered up the steps to the third floor of the science building. In the student assistants' lounge he was relieved to see that Kayla was already there at her desk looking at a series of diagrams. Gary was standing close behind her looking over her shoulder. "Hey," Andy called as he came in.

"Hey, Andy. How's it going?"

"Not so good," Andy replied. "I need to talk to Lisa, but I haven't been able to contact her since yesterday. Have either of you seen her recently?

They looked at each other and shrugged. "Nope. Not since yesterday. She was here a little after noon," said Gary.

"Yeah," added Kayla. "She was looking for you. We told her that you had gone off with Cynthia."

"With Cynthia! Oh geez," said Andy, rolling his eyes.

"Yeah, she thought that was real interesting," said Kayla, enjoying Andy's discomfort. Then she added, "She said she was going to go see that guy in the Safety Office and show him the notebook that you found. Didn't she tell you?"

"No. I haven't heard from her since yesterday morning." Andy slumped in his chair. Then, sitting forward, he addressed the others. "Look. You know that we found Jodi's notebook, and it proves that Rathburn was having her make Ecstasy, and maybe even shows that he purposely tried to injure her. We're not entirely sure. But now Lisa's missing!"

"Missing?" said Gary.

"Yeah, look. Her notebooks are still on her desk, just the way they were last night. Nobody I know has seen or heard from her since you did yesterday." Andy looked from one to the other. "Guys, I'm really worried that something may have happened to her. You say that she went to see Davis, the campus safety guy?"

"Yeah, she said something about now maybe he'd believe her, since she had that notebook."

"Well, I guess I should go check with him," said Andy starting to get up.

Their conversation was interrupted as Jamie burst into the room. "Whoa, guys. I just saw Rathburn coming down the hall to his office. You should see him!" he exclaimed.

"Rathburn!" spat Andy. "I bet he's behind this."

"What are you talking about?" asked Kayla.

"Why? Was he in drag?" joked Gary.

"Nothing like that!" Jamie laughed. "Somebody must have socked him a good one. He's got two black eyes. He looks like a ghoul!"

"Couldn't have happened to a more deserving person," said Kayla.

"Wish it'd been me that did it," said Gary rubbing his knuckles.

"He deserves more than a black eye after all he's done," declared Andy. "I bet he knows where Lisa is. I'm gonna go ask him. Come on." Andy started for the door. Gary and Kayla followed. Not sure what was going to happen, Jamie brought up the rear. They trooped the length of the hall and stopped outside Rathburn's closed door. Andy stepped up and knocked.

The door was yanked open, and Professor Rathburn glared out at him. "What do you want?" he demanded.

The spectacle of Rathburn's damaged face and the vehemence of his response caused Andy to step back. "Ah… ah… we're looking for Lisa Ross. Do you know where she is?"

"No idea," he stated flatly and started to shut the door.

"Another false negative, methinks," called Jamie from the back of the group.

Andy felt his anger and frustration return. "Wait a minute," he said stepping forward and preventing the door from closing. "We know that you were having Jodi Sanders make Ecstasy in the lab. And we know that you told her to add something that made her reaction explode, nearly killing her. Lisa knew that. And now she's missing! What have you done with her? What did you do to her?" By this time Andy was nearly shouting and several passing students were stopping to watch.

Rathburn stepped toward Andy menacingly, forcing him back into the hallway. "Shut up, you little twerp," he hissed, "You… you've no…" But then he paused, as a look of genuine surprise crossed his bruised countenance. "Wait, you said…Lisa Ross…is missing?"

"Yeah. Where is she?"

Rathburn looked around at the growing number of witnesses to the scene that was playing out. Coming to some personal realization he looked down and brought his hand to his head. "Oh shit," he muttered. Then, regaining his composure, he straightened up, and addressed Andy and the crowd of onlookers, "All of you, get out of here! Go! Get out of here or I'll… I'll… see that you're all expelled." Rathburn retreated into his office and slammed the door.

"Can he do that?" one student asked. "Have us expelled?"

"Not even possible," scoffed another.

"Good grief! What happened to him?" asked a third.

"Looks like he was in a fight."

"I would have liked to have seen that," said another.

The crowd lingered for a few minutes waiting to see whether anything more was going to happen. However, Rathburn's door stayed closed, and the students gradually wandered away. Andy remained, looking at the closed door and wondering whether he should try knocking again and attempt to pressure Rathburn for a better answer. The crowd had largely dispersed, and Andy felt his resolve failing. As he turned to go back to the student assistants' lounge, he saw Cynthia standing against the wall across from Rathburn's door. She signaled to him to come over and then fell in walking beside him.

"Andy," she began softly.

"Yeah?"

She looked around checking to make sure that nobody else was listening.

"Promise me that if anything comes of this, you didn't hear it from me, okay?" She waited for his reply.

"Okay, I promise," agreed Andy.

She hesitated, apparently pondering whether to continue. She squinted at Andy. "I'm not sure if this might be helpful, but Charles, I mean Professor Rathburn, has something going on with some people that he meets at a little bar called the Sea Shanty Saloon up on Banks St. The guys he hangs with there are rather… well, not so nice, to say the least. I don't know for sure, but I'm thinking that they might have something to do with all of this."

Andy stopped walking and considered Cynthia warily as he thought about what she had said. "Thanks," he said uncertainly.

"Remember, you didn't hear it from me." She turned and walked in the opposite direction. Andy mulled over what Cynthia had told him and returned to the assistants' lounge. A new plan of action was formulating in his mind.

In the lounge Gary and Kayla had gone back to their desks. "Hey guys, have you got some time?" Andy asked as he came in. "I want to go hunt for Lisa. And I've got an idea where we can look. Will you help me?"

Gary looked up. "Yeah, absolutely. I've got time, until one o'clock. That's my next lecture."

"I'm in," agreed Kayla promptly, shutting her notebook and grabbing her coat.

"So, what's the plan?" Gary asked as the three of them descended the stairs to the exit.

"First, I think that we should drop in on the campus safety guy, Mr. Davis," said Andy. "That's the last place that we know that she was going." They paused and looked around. The campus safety office was at the south end of campus while Gary's jeep was parked in the commuter lot on the east side.

"Okay," said Gary. They pivoted and walked south.

When they entered the safety office, they found the program assistant,

Marion Atkinson, seated behind the counter and a student assistant working at a nearby desk. Andy approached the reception counter. "Hello," he began, "we'd like to talk to Mr. Davis."

Marion looked them over sternly and asked, "What's this about?"

Andy hesitated not wanting to recount the whole story. "We think that a crime has been committed on campus, and we'd like to talk to Mr. Davis."

Marion paused, wondering whether she could elicit some interesting details. "Well, he's not here right now."

Andy shifted on his feet and glanced at Gary and Kayla. "Do you know when he'll be back?"

Marion's visage softened as she decided to be more cooperative. "Actually, no, I don't know. He was supposed to be here this morning at eight, but he hasn't shown up." She glanced up at a large clock on the wall. "And he hasn't called in, so we just don't know when to expect him." She looked at the student assistant who returned her look with a shrug.

"Okay. Thanks anyway," said Andy nodding. He turned to Kayla and Gary. "So, I guess we move on." They headed out the door and turned in the direction of the commuter lot where Gary's jeep was parked.

"Now what?" asked Kayla.

"Next, let's go by Lisa's apartment," said Andy. "I want to check on something that I should have done yesterday."

"What's that?"

"I want to see if her car is still there."

"Okay."

When they arrived at Gary's jeep, they spent the first few minutes consolidating the variety of items that littered his back seat and floor and carrying several loads to a trash barrel that was placed at the edge of the lot. Gary drove the few blocks to Lisa's apartment, while Andy once again confirmed that calling her cellphone number only produced a diversion to voicemail. Pulling up in front, Andy jumped out and went up to the door. This time there was no answer at all to his knocking. He came back to the jeep and spoke to Kayla and Gary. "I'm going around back. There's a garage back there where I think Lisa keeps her car most of the time. Why don't you drive around to the alley."

The garage was big enough for two cars. Andy tried the service door and found it unlocked. Peering inside he could barely make out the outlines of two cars in the darkness. He felt for a switch on the wall, flipped it and a single light bulb hanging from a cord in the middle of the ceiling came on. There in the far stall was

Lisa's white Toyota Avalon.

Andy switched off the light and closed the door behind him. Coming around the corner of the garage he found Gary's jeep idling in the alley. He got into the back seat. "Her car is there, which means that she hasn't driven home or gone off somewhere," he stated.

"So?" Kayla queried.

"Okay. Here's what I think," said Andy. "Rathburn figured out that Lisa knew too much about his drug making and his sabotage of Jodi's reaction. So, he and whoever he is working with have kidnapped her, and… done something with her." Andy found it hard to think about what that something might be. "The one lead that I have is that Rathburn meets these other people at a place called the Sea Shanty Saloon. So, let's find this place and see what we can dig up."

"I know that place," said Gary, and he put his jeep in gear.

"Is a bar going to be open at this time in the morning?" asked Kayla.

Gary looked over at her. "Well, we're going to find out."

In a few minutes they were approaching the Sea Shanty on Banks St. Gary pulled to a stop in front. The street appeared to be almost completely deserted. Across the street was a large grey corrugated metal warehouse with bright red letters spelling out K-A-M, Koreo Amerain Mercantile. A couple of dusty older model cars were in the dirt parking lot south of the warehouse. Andy got out and went to the door and tried it but found it locked. The neon beer sign in the window was turned off. He looked up and down the street and then went back to sit in Gary's jeep. The day was overcast, the sky a uniform light grey color and the wind from the west was chilling.

"Okay. Now what?" asked Kayla.

"Let's go around back," suggested Gary. "I know where there's a back door."

"Yeah, but is that any more likely to be unlocked?" said Kayla.

"Maybe," said Gary lightly. He started the engine and looked over his shoulder. Before he could pull away from the curb, however, a bright red sporty car roared past.

"Hey. Is that Rathburn's car?" Andy exclaimed. They watched the receding vehicle as it sped down the street and turned sharply in at the north end of the large warehouse.

"Where do you suppose he's going in such a hurry?" asked Kayla.

"Let's find out," said Gary. He pulled away from the curb and proceeded slowly up the street. "You guys look. I'm going to keep moving." Gary drove slowly past the end of the warehouse and turned away at the next corner.

"It's Rathburn, all right," said Andy. "His car was parked there, and he was standing at the service door like he's waiting to get in."

"So, what can we do?" asked Kayla.

"If Lisa is in there, we have to get her out," said Andy.

"Hold on, guys," said Gary. "We can't just go barging in the front door and expect that whoever is in there is just going to give up without a fight. I say we sneak in the back door and find out what's going on and who we are dealing with before we try to do anything."

"Okay," the others agreed. Gary circled the block and pulled into the parking lot that bordered the south end of the KAM warehouse. Whereas the north end of the warehouse had featured two large overhead doors for vehicles, this end had only a single service door off to one side. Gary turned off his engine and they looked at the warehouse wall.

"I don't suppose that door is unlocked, do you?" Andy asked.

"Probably not," said Gary, "but why don't you go and check." Then he added, "Walk up the sidewalk to that corner, and then stay along the wall. I don't see any security cameras, but just in case, ya know?"

Andy got out and approached the service door while Gary and Kayla sat and watched from the car. Although it was mid-morning, nobody seemed to be about. Trying the door Andy found it locked. He stuck his hands in his coat pockets and sauntered back to the car.

Gary got out and went around and opened the back of his jeep. After rummaging around among bags and boxes and loose tools, he came up with a small cloth package. Kayla and Andy looked at each other questioningly.

"What?" said Andy.

"Just wait, you'll see," Gary replied. After a little more rummaging he came up with a roll of duct tape and handed it to Kayla. "You never know when you might need some duct tape," he said with a wry smile.

They walked as a group to the service door where Gary knelt down and spread his package open on the concrete in front of them. Unrolled, the cloth contained an assortment of metal rods and wires. Gary picked up a couple, held them together and inserted them into the keyhole of the lock on the door.

"Oh!" exclaimed Kayla. "Lock picks."

"Is this legal?" asked Andy.

Gary gave him a sidelong glance. "Is what they are doing to Lisa legal?"

Andy nodded, but then looked around to check again whether there were any spectators in sight.

"Where did you learn how to do this?" Kayla asked, the surprise showing in her voice.

"My dad worked for a while as a locksmith," he explained nonchalantly. "So, he showed me a few things."

Gary fiddled with the lock, trying several different combinations of wires and rods without success. Kayla and Andy shifted on their feet looking around and feeling nervous. Suddenly there was a click. "Got it," said Gary with a tone of satisfaction. He turned the handle of the door and it opened. Propping it open a few inches with his foot he turned to Kayla, "Can you peel off a couple pieces of that tape about six inches long?" Gary took the pieces offered to him and applied them over the latch. "Don't want to get locked in," he explained. "Just in case." Turning to the others, he asked, "Ready?"

Kayla and Andy looked at him wide-eyed. "I think so," said Andy.

Chapter 25   2016, April 19, Tuesday

Gary stuffed his tools into his jacket pocket and looked at the others. "Okay, here's how we do this. Walk slowly and quietly. Don't say anything unless it's absolutely necessary. If you see something, just point. Keep track of where we go in there. This is our only way out that we know of, so remember how to get back here if you need to exit in a hurry. Okay?"

"Okay," they both agreed.

"Kayla, do you have your phone on you?"

She nodded.

"Keep it ready. If we find something, or if something happens, take pictures. And make sure the sound is off." Kayla checked her phone and stuffed it into her jacket pocket. Andy did the same.

"Oh. And if we get confronted, spread out, move away from each other. And if it gets really dangerous, then just run like hell. Get out and get help. Got it?"

They both nodded solemnly. Gary slowly opened the door just far enough for them all to slip in and let it close softly behind them.

"Just stand here a minute," Gary said in a low tone. "Wait for your eyes to adjust to the dark."

There was enough light coming from elsewhere in the building that gradually they could readily make out their surroundings. The smooth concrete floor of the warehouse was stacked with boxes, wrapped in plastic and arranged on pallets in rows with aisles between the stacks that would be wide enough to maneuver a forklift. Light seemed to be coming from the far end of the warehouse. Gary led them along the south wall farthest from the light. As they moved behind a row of pallets, their view was cut off, but then, as they came in line with the next aisle, they could see to the far end of the building where the source of the light was located. Reaching the far side of the building Gary turned and led them along the wall in the direction of the light. Walking slowly and quietly in the shadows, they came to the end of the last stack of boxes and stopped. Here they could see that the light was coming from a glass-walled office at the end of the building. The office was fairly large; it held several desks and a bank of five or six filing cabinets. Charts and schedule boards bedecked the far wall. Between them and the office lay about thirty feet of bare concrete floor that was partially lit by the fluorescent lights that illuminated the interior of the office. They paused and listened but could hear no sound.

Gary signaled them to walk cautiously from the shadows by the side wall where they were standing, toward the door to the office. When they had taken just a few steps they were able to see inside through the glass. There, sitting slumped on a chair was Lisa. It was difficult to tell that it was her at first. Her arms were behind her apparently bound. Her hair was disheveled, hanging about her head that was resting down on her chest. Andy gave a start when he saw her and started to call out, but Gary raised his hand. As they took a few steps closer, they could see a second figure in the room. A large man with a shaved head was seated at a desk paging through a magazine. Thick muscled arms were revealed by the rolled-up sleeves of his plaid lumberjack shirt.

Gary turned around and pushed them back into the shadows. "Wait. Let's think about this," he said softly. Suddenly, as if on cue, a door in the partition wall adjacent to the office burst open and two men came walking briskly around the corner toward the office. The first one they recognized as Steven Davis, the Burlington Campus Security Officer, and the second was Professor Rathburn. Rathburn looked haggard and was pleading with Davis. "Look, Steven. This is more than I ever bargained for."

"Yeah, well, nobody asked you to hire students who are going to figure out what's going on," Davis retorted.

"I had no idea this was going to happen, but…" Rathburn paused to look through the windows at Lisa sitting slumped in the chair. "Look. Making Ecstasy is one thing, but murder, Steven?!"

Davis whirled on Rathburn, addressing him fiercely. "You are the one that brought these two into this, and you are going to be the one to get rid of them. Got it? One way or another."

"But I just can't," whined Rathburn. Their conversation became indistinct as they moved into the office.

Gary faced Andy and Kayla and murmured quick instructions. "Andy, go stand by those boxes over there across from the office. When I signal, call out to Lisa. If they chase you, just run for the door where we came in. It probably won't come to that. When they come out, I'll give them a little surprise. Kayla, stay in the shadows here. Video this if you want. Okay? Everybody ready?" They nodded in reply. Gary walked quickly and quietly to the shadows around the corner where the front wall of the office ended. When he was in position, he pointed at Andy and nodded.

Andy moved to the end of the aisle across the open space from the doorway to the office. Stepping forward a few feet into the light, he called out loudly, "Lisa? Lisa? Where are you?"

The men inside the office looked up in alarm and moved to the doorway. Davis came out first and started walking toward Andy menacingly; Rathburn followed but stopped a short distance outside the office door.

"Who are you? What are you doing here?" Davis bellowed at Andy.

"I, I, I'm looking for Lisa," he managed to stammer backing away.

Peeking around the corner and watching through the glass, Gary saw that the man in the plaid shirt had opened a drawer in one of the desks. When his hand came out, he was holding a pistol. He quickly followed after the others.

As the plaid-shirted man cleared the doorway, Gary moved. With three rapid steps he closed the distance and delivered a sharp side kick to the man's knee. An unpleasant snapping sound was heard as the man screamed and his leg crumpled under him. As he fell in the direction of his damaged leg, Gary pivoted, bringing the flat of his forearm in a solid strike to the side of the man's head. With a resounding smack the burly man completed his journey to the ground and lay still. The pistol clattered harmlessly to the floor.

Hearing the noise behind him, Davis whirled around. Seeing his compatriot slumped on the ground he protested. "Hey, you can't…" he began, taking a step menacingly in Gary's direction. Gary walked toward Davis and with lightning speed delivered a front kick to his solar plexus. Davis fell backwards clutching his chest. Doubled over on the ground, he wheezed struggling to breathe.

Andy and Gary stood and watched the two fallen figures uncertain whether the threat was gone. Gary stepped to the pistol and pushed it off to one side with his toe. "We'll just leave that there for now," he said.

Meanwhile, Rathburn, who had been witnessing the events from just outside the office door, started edging toward the service door in the partition. Kayla stepped from the shadows and intercepted him. "I don't think that you should leave just yet," she said.

"Get out of my way," he hissed. Attempting to force his way past her, he swung his fist at her head. Kayla saw it coming and easily ducked. Training kicked in, and she came back with an upward thrust of the heel of her hand to Rathburn's chin. Rathburn crumpled to the ground and groaned, blood trickling from his mouth.

Gary came over to Kayla. "Gosh, you're beautiful," he said in admiration.

"I've got a good teacher," she replied smiling.

Getting serious again, Gary grabbed Rathburn by his coat and dragged him closer to the other two men on the ground. "Still got that duct tape?" he asked Kayla.

"Right here, boss," she said pulling the roll from her jacket.

The three students applied long strips of duct tape to the semi-conscious men on the ground, securing their wrists behind them. "Andy, go check on Lisa. Kayla and I will finish this," said Gary.

Andy ran back into the office and knelt by the body tied to the chair. "Lisa! Lisa! Are you okay?" She raised her head groggily and moaned. He pushed her hair back from her face. A purplish bruise covered one cheek and her eye on that side was swollen shut. "Oh, Lisa!" he exclaimed. Dried blood encrusted her upper lip and her lips looked swollen. He went around to the back of her chair and began working the knots loose. When her hands were freed, he moved to her side to keep her from falling off the chair. "Come on, Lisa. Let's get out of here." But Lisa was in no condition to stand or walk. Andy held her in his arms as consciousness slowly came back. Lisa put her arms around Andy's shoulders. "Oh, Andy! You found me! I thought…" She began to sob quietly.

Outside the office, Gary and Kayla stood watch over their captives on the floor. Kayla was trying to call the police, tapping numbers on her phone. "Reception's not great in here," she muttered. Then a voice came through. "Ah, hello. Ah, yah. Could you send somebody over here, please? Um, well, we have got some kidnappers, yeah, and I think they are also selling drugs, um, a couple of guys are lying on the floor, and there is a girl who, ah, is not well." There was a pause. "Yeah. My name is Kayla Martin. Ah, no, I don't live in Superior. I'm a student at Burlington. Yeah. Ah…" She held the phone away from her mouth. "Gary. Where are we?”

"We're in the KAM warehouse across the street from the Sea Shanty near 5th and Banks. Tell them that the service door on the south end of the building is unlocked."

Kayla relayed the information. "Yeah, yeah, well hurry, one of them had a gun and he's probably gonna wake up soon." She ended the call. "I'm not sure that he believed me." She stared at the inert bodies on the floor and rolled her eyes.

They waited for what seemed like an hour but was probably only ten minutes until they heard sirens outside the building. Then the door they had come in at the far end of the warehouse banged open and the police could be heard approaching. Three blue-uniformed officers stepped into the open space in front of the office with their weapons drawn.

"No need for weapons, officer," Gary called while simultaneously raising his hands. "It's all under control." The policemen surveyed the scene and lowered and holstered their weapons.

"Who called us?" the first one asked.

Kayla stepped forward. "I did, sir." Kayla explained how they had been concerned about their friend Lisa, how they had entered the building – skipping the part about Gary's picking the lock – how they had found Lisa in the office, and the confrontation with Davis and the plaid-shirted man.

"So, who is this?" one of the officers asked, indicating Rathburn.

"I'm Professor Charles Rathburn," he said struggling unsuccessfully to get to his feet, "and I demand to have my lawyer present."

"And he is probably responsible for manufacturing a lot of illegal drugs," interjected Gary. Rathburn glared at him.

"Oh, really," responded one of the other officers stepping closer. "McNeill will want to hear about this." To Rathburn he said, "Don't go anywhere. You can call your lawyer from the station." The officer stepped back keeping an eye on the captives and started talking into his radio.

Gary tapped one of the officers on the shoulder and pointed to the gun on the floor. "You'll probably want to take care of that, too," he said.

The officer who seemed to be in charge spoke to the others. "Okay, let's get all these folks down to the station. Call for medical, too. We've got a couple here who don't seem to be too healthy."

Everything seemed to happen very slowly after that. More sirens were heard outside; more police officers appeared. Medical technicians arrived. Lisa was helped onto a gurney and covered with a blanket. Andy watched as they took her away.

"Where will they take her?"

"They'll take her to Memorial on south Tower," one of the policemen replied.

Davis and Rathburn, who were both recovered enough to walk, were escorted out separately, and the third man, grimacing in pain with an oddly shaped leg, was wheeled out on a gurney. Finally, the three students were ushered into the back of two police cars and driven to Police Headquarters.

Chapter 26   2016, April 19, Tuesday

Later that afternoon, Andy, Gary and Kayla were ushered into a bleak interview room at Police Headquarters. The pale mint green walls and dented grey metal furniture did little to diminish the exhilaration that they felt from having survived the events at the KAM warehouse. The young-looking blonde police officer, who Andy recognized as Chris Jenkins, the officer who had interviewed him and Lisa several days ago, indicated chairs where the students could sit. Earlier, when the three had arrived at Police Headquarters, they were told that they needed to make statements. Initially each of them had been interviewed in private, but then they were collected into this room.

"Hey team, we did all right," commented Gary as they assembled.

"Yeah, we did," agreed Kayla.

"Thanks, guys," Andy said to the two of them.

"Do you think Henderson is going to excuse me from my one o'clock?" Gary said with a wry smile referring to his missed afternoon class.

Andy smiled and then addressed Officer Jenkins, "So. What's next?"

"Just a few more questions, if you don't mind," Jenkins replied as he went to the door and admitted an older man in a rumpled suit. "This is Mr. Terrence O'Neil. He's with the DEA, that's the federal Drug Enforcement Administration. They are the organization that…"

"I think we have a good idea of what they do," Gary cut in. "Let's just get on with it."

"Okay," Jenkins replied and turned to O'Neill.

O'Neill, who had not been present during any of the previous interviews, stepped forward. "So, I've been told that one of you thinks that somebody involved in this…" he waved his hand in what might have been the direction of the KAM warehouse, "…event today, was manufacturing illegal drugs?"

"Yes, officer," Andy jumped in. "Actually, the person who figured it out was Lisa, the girl who was taken to the hospital. She and I found the evidence in the debris that was left over from Jodi's explosion. Oh. Yeah." He paused, remembering what they had also uncovered about that earlier event. "Yeah, and we also think that Professor Rathburn may have sabotaged Jodi's reaction, too, which caused the explosion that put her in the hospital. Oh, this isn't coming out very organized, is it?"

"Take your time, take your time," said O'Neill smiling slightly at Andy's flustered explanation.

Over the next half hour Andy recounted the events in a slower more methodical sequence. He described how they had identified the materials in Jodi's reaction, and how that had led them to conclude that Rathburn was synthesizing Ecstasy and purposely tried to harm Jodi by directing her to put an explosive chemical into her reaction. Then he described how they had tried to find Lisa, who had been kidnapped, and how that had led them to be at the KAM warehouse. He decided to leave out mentioning the vital tip he had gotten from Cynthia.

O'Neill listened carefully, occasionally writing something on a notepad. "Very nice," he commented as he clicked his pen and closed his notebook. "This really helps. We have been tracking a number of drug shipments back to this area, but we haven't been able to pinpoint the source. Until now," he added. Turning to Jenkins he said, "Okay. I've got all that I need, for now." To the students he said, "Don't any of you take any vacations soon. I'm going to be checking out everything that you told me, so if I need to talk to you again, I'll be giving you a call. Okay?" Addressing Jenkins he said, "Unless you need something more, I'm done with these kids."

"Nope. I'm all done." Turning to the students he said, "That's it. You can go. And thanks for your help. You did well."

"Thank you," Kayla replied. "But before we go, could you tell us what's going to happen to those guys in the warehouse?"

Jenkins paused. "Well, I'm not sure how many charges are going to be brought against each of them, but O'Neill thinks that all of them were involved in the drug manufacturing and distribution. So that probably means prison time. Then, there was the kidnapping, so somebody will get charged with that. And then, there could be charges of attempted murder if that lab explosion was really planned and not just an accident. So, depending on who gets which charge, I'd guess it means quite a few years in prison. But nothing is for sure until the lawyers and judge are done."

"Wow," Kayla muttered, nodding.

Outside on the sidewalk, they squinted in the bright sunshine of a warm April afternoon. "They could have at least given us a ride back to my jeep," Gary commented.

"No worries," Kayla chimed in. "It's not far. We can hoof it."

It was almost four p.m. when the three set off back in the direction of the Sea Shanty where Gary had left his jeep. The fresh air and sunshine, their release from the police station, and the growing realization that they had successfully freed Lisa from her kidnappers and put a stop to Rathburn's drug operation buoyed their spirits.

"Jeez, I'm hungry," admitted Gary, "anybody want to stop by the Burger Box?"

"Absolutely!" responded Kayla.

Andy thought for a minute. "I'd really like to get to Memorial and find out what's up with Lisa." They walked in silence for a few steps, and then Andy said, "On the other hand, yeah. I need some food. I'll catch up with Lisa after."

After a questionably nutritious but nevertheless filling meal, Gary dropped Andy off at his apartment. Without going in, he circled around to the parking area and got into his old green Escort. The drive to Memorial Hospital was familiar, but this time his concern for what awaited him was more poignant. He checked in at the reception desk and rode the elevator to the same floor Jodi Sanders had occupied. He turned in at Lisa's door and knocked gently.

"Come in," came the response.

Andy pushed the door open to find Lisa sitting up in bed, a magazine that she had been reading lay in her lap.

"Oh, Andy! Come here!" She held out her arms.

Andy quickly stepped to her bedside and they embraced. Lisa held him tightly for several minutes. When she finally released him, he could see that her eyes were brimming with tears. "Oh, Andy," she gasped, "I was so scared. I thought they were going to kill me!"

"I know. I know. I was so worried. I didn't know where you'd gone. I didn't know if I would ever see you again." They held each other as well as they could with Lisa propped up in the bed. Finally Andy took a step back, but continued to hold her hand. She had been cleaned up, and her hair had been washed and combed and dried. Even so, the bruise on her cheek was swollen and discolored, and a cut in her lip still had the look of dried blood. But otherwise, she was awake and appeared to have her faculties about her.

"How did you know where to find me? I don't remember anything after going to see Mr. Davis."

"Actually, it was Cynthia who gave me the clue. She knew that Rathburn hung out at that Sea Shanty bar and sent us there. Then we saw his car at the warehouse." Andy told Lisa the whole story of their plan to rescue her, how finally the police had come, and all the time that they spent getting interviewed at the station. "I think that the police believe us now," he concluded with a wry smile. Andy stepped closer and gave Lisa another embrace. "Well, you're safe now, and you're going to be okay," he said.

A knock at the door startled them to separate abruptly. "Lisa?" came a soft voice at the door.

"Mom!" cried Lisa.

Mrs. Ross, wearing slacks, a puffy purple ski jacket and oversized sunglasses perched on her white knit stocking cap, came into the room in a rush and displaced Andy from Lisa's side. "Oh, honey!" she exclaimed, "Look at you. Oh, goodness. What did they do to you? Oh, honey!" Mrs. Sanders held Lisa's face in her hands and kissed her repeatedly.

"Mom, mom! Stop, already. I'm okay."

"Are you? Oh. I've been driving all afternoon. I left as soon as they called. I've been so worried. Are you sure you're okay? Where are the doctors?" Mrs. Ross finally slowed down enough to look around the room. She took in Andy's presence without comment.

"Set your stuff over there," instructed Lisa. "Mom, this is Andy Treydon. I think that I introduced you once before when you were here."

"Hello, Andy," she said stiffly, as she discarded her jacket, hat, and sunglasses on a chair in the corner.

Aware of her mother's aloofness toward Andy, Lisa said, "You should know, Mom, that Andy is the one who rescued me."

Andy looked at the floor shyly, "Well, Gary and Kayla were there, too, and…" he trailed off.

Mrs. Ross regarded Andy with a slightly greater degree of warmth. "Well, thank you, Andy. I want to hear all about it." Turning back to Lisa, she said, "But first, how soon can we get you out of here? And where are the doctors? I want to speak to somebody in charge."

"Mom! Relax. I can ring for the nurse, and she can give you the official story if you want. But I can tell you that they would like to have me stay in here overnight just for observation. A real nice Dr. Halvorsen was in here earlier, and she checked me all over. These bruises are going to heal okay. Because they gave me some drug that knocked me out, they want to watch me for a while just to make sure there are no lasting effects. She'll be back tomorrow morning and then I'll probably get released. Okay?"

"Hmmpf," said Mrs. Ross, barely mollified. Again, she surveyed the room and allowed her gaze to settle on Andy a little longer. Then she went back to Lisa's side and held her face. "Oh, honey. I'm so glad that you are okay." She kissed her again and released her. Straightening up she said, "Well, first I'm going to visit the 'necessary' room, and then I better find out where I'm going to stay tonight." She proceeded out the door and left Andy and Lisa in silence.

Andy returned to Lisa's bedside and held her hand. "Well, I hate to leave you, Lis, but it's been kind of a long day. And, I'm afraid that I have a whole lot that I'm supposed to have ready for tomorrow. Do you think that you will be coming back to campus tomorrow?"

"I plan to," she replied, stroking the back of Andy's hand. "I imagine that Mom will be here when I get released, and if she'll let me go, I can probably talk her into dropping me by campus."

"Sounds good," Andy nodded. "Send me a text when you get on campus. I'll come meet you. Okay?" Reflecting for a moment he said, "Your mom certainly has a force about her."

Lisa chuckled and then smiled slyly at Andy. "You know, when we get married, you're going to have to stand up to that."

Andy's eyes widened. "What? What did you say?"

"Come here and give me a kiss," she said laughing, "and then go away. I've got to rest."

Andy stepped over to the bed, looked her in the eyes and kissed her. "I love you, Lisa. See you tomorrow."

Riding home in his car, Andy's thoughts were soaring. "Yeah! Maybe this is all going to work out all right. Yeah!"

Chapter 27

Epilogue
2017, May 6, Saturday

Wearing a new pair of jeans and a new plaid shirt, Andy left the NMR lab between the basements of Smith and Kolthoff Halls at noon and walked across the mall of the University of Minnesota campus in the direction of the Fresh Food Co-op at the corner of Washington and Ontario. The early May day was aglow with warmth and sunshine; leaves were breaking out on the trees and the grass was turning green everywhere. The smell of warm, wet earth was in the air, and students were chatting at outdoor tables, and playing frisbee on the mall. At the co-op, Andy was greeted by the familiar faces of several workers who had come to recognize him as a regular shopper. After lingering over the fresh produce, he purchased some mushrooms, peppers, onions, tomatoes, beans, and ground beef, and then proceeded to the corner of University and Huron where he caught one of the frequent buses that brought hordes of students to and from the campus daily. A short five-minute ride down University Avenue brought him to a large brick apartment building that had at one time been a commercial establishment, but recently had been partitioned into modern apartments. An elevator took him to the fourth floor where he unlocked the door to the two-bedroom apartment that he shared with Lisa and Mariah. "Hello," he called as he entered, but, as he suspected, he was the first one home. He set his groceries in the kitchen and shed his backpack in the bedroom that he and Lisa occupied.

Andy and Lisa had proposed to each other shortly after graduation a year ago, but they had decided not to set a wedding date right away. They were still in what they called their "trial period" ostensibly to see how well they were going to be able to balance their marriage plans with their developing careers. Mariah was totally devoted to her graduate studies, spent long hours on campus, largely stayed out of Lisa and Andy's way, and was quite unperturbed by their presence whenever she was at home. In fact, her independence sometimes made it difficult to arrange a time when they could do something together.

On this day, Andy had taken the afternoon to prepare a large batch of his personal recipe for chili, which was to be the main dish for dinner at which a couple of special guests were to be present. Several hours later, despite the open windows that admitted the fresh spring breezes, the apartment was filled with mouth-watering aromas. As he finished preparing a salad and setting the dining table for five, the intercom beeped. Andy buzzed the visitors in and moments later he was opening the apartment door for Gary and Kayla. "Mr. and Mrs. Pollan, how nice to see you," he greeted them. Kayla gave Andy a hug and Gary and Andy shook hands. Gary was carrying a large carton that Andy directed him to take to the kitchen.

"We were up in Hayward last weekend to see Kayla's folks," Gary explained, "so we brought back a couple of cases of New Glarus Spotted Cow. It's been on ice in a cooler in my car all afternoon, so we can open some now, if you want."

"Wonderful!" responded Andy. "This will go great with tonight's dinner." He popped the caps on three of the bottles and transferred the rest into the refrigerator.

"Nice apartment," commented Kayla from the other room. The three moved into the main living room where they admired the décor. A north-east corner featured windows on two sides that mostly overlooked the businesses that lined University Avenue, but nevertheless afforded expansive views. Other walls sported a couple of framed posters of bygone rock bands. Two matching couches that appeared to be in good condition and a coffee table and some reading lamps completed the sitting area. The dining area included a solid-looking extendable table with four wooden chairs. A fifth folding chair had been added to accommodate tonight's group. A rather elaborate chandelier centered over the table was the only element that seemed somewhat out-of-place among the rest of the nascent yuppie accoutrements.

"It came with the apartment," explained Andy when he saw Kayla eyeing it doubtfully.

"You guys look real settled," murmured Kayla. Turning to Gary while examining a reading lamp next to one of the couches, she said, "We should get something like this, don't you think?"

Gary inspected the lamp's switch and its dual up-and-down facing LED lights. "Where'd you get this, Andy, IKEA?"

"I'm not sure," Andy answered. "Lisa's folks had a lot of this stuff, and they are just letting us use it until, well, pretty much indefinitely. Not sure where they got it."

"How is all that going? You and her folks, I mean," asked Kayla.

"It's really going pretty well, actually," said Andy. "Her dad is really laid-back, easy-going. I think he likes me fine. And her mom is warming up a little, I guess. Maybe. I think that she is at least starting to believe that I might possibly be a suitable life companion for Lisa and really be able to make her happy. And maybe even earn enough to keep her properly fed and clothed."

Kayla scoffed softly, "Yeah, I guess. Ha."

The three of them chatted, sipping their beers and exchanging information about their new lives while Andy finished setting the table. Then the door opened, and Lisa and Mariah trooped into the room. "Hey Kayla, Gary," they called as they saw the others.

"Come on in," called Andy as he headed for the kitchen. "The beer is cold and the chili is hot!" Mariah and Lisa deposited their belongings in their rooms and returned to distribute greetings and hugs. Minutes later they were all seated at the table while Andy served steaming bowls of chili with crackers, cheese and chopped onions.

As they started to dig in, Lisa said, "Kayla, it's so good to see you. I really like what you've done with your hair." Indeed, Kayla's long reddish-brown hair had been seriously trimmed to a chin-length style."

"Yeah, thanks. It helps me keep my hands free," she chuckled. Changing the subject, she said, "So, everybody, I want an update on what you all are doing."

Andy replied first. "Well, I'm working as a technician for Professor Coyle at the U, running several different instruments in his lab. I'm getting a lot of experience, and I really like the work. It's soft money, right now, but I think the skills will be very transferable if and when I move in the future."

Andy looked to Lisa who added, "Mariah and I are both mostly doing coursework. We'll be taking qualifying exams, probably in the fall. In the meantime, we are rotating through several different professors' labs. Lately I've been getting interested in the total synthesis of natural products, but we'll see if that continues."

"Lisa said it," agreed Mariah, "it's mostly coursework right now. Recently I've been working in Khalid's lab, in molecular pharmacology, and she is doing receptor isolation for brain neurotransmitters. I think that would be a really cool field to work in. But nothing's been decided yet."

"So, can you explain to us how Ecstasy causes its effects?" asked Gary.

"Absolutely. Come back next year and I'll have it all deciphered for you," she chuckled, and then asked, "So how about you two?"

"There was a little misunderstanding with one company last spring, but that all got worked out and now I'm working with the Minnesota Bureau of Criminal Apprehension, the BCA, and it is just great," said Gary. "It seems like every day there is a new challenge: new case, new evidence, some new thing that has to be figured out. The biggest problem is that everything, and I mean everything, has to be documented. Evidence has to be handled according to protocols, double signed for, and kept under lock and key. That part is a pain, but the problem-solving part is fun."

"Sounds really interesting," said Andy. "Do you ever get to do any field work?"

"Yeah, actually. Sometimes we go out to crime scenes to collect evidence. But I don't do any of that on my own. I'm still junior grade, so I am always under the supervision of a senior investigator. Someday, though…"

"So, you don't ever have to do battle with any criminals?" Lisa said smiling. "I know you'd be good at it."

"I just have to keep a few of my talents hidden," said Gary, trying to sound mysterious. "They are more potent when they come as a surprise, don't you know."

"Well, I'm very grateful for your hidden talents, Mr. Pollan." said Lisa seriously.

"How about you, Kayla?" broke in Mariah.

"Well, I've been doing some lab tech work for Apex BioMed in Bloomington. It has been kinda repetitive. Mostly preparing solutions and a lot of routine chromatography. Quality control stuff, you know. But I'm thinking that I'm going to be looking for something different. Maybe. We'll see. Nothing's for sure, right now."

Gary stepped in. "We are thinking that Mrs. Pollan here might be taking on a new job in the not-so-distant future." Smiling, he reached over and took her hand.

There was a pause around the table. Then, "You mean? You mean?" Lisa exclaimed.

"No," Kayla assured her, "not yet, but we're thinking, maybe…"

Smiles and knowing nods were exchanged around the table as each member contemplated the implied news. Breaking the pause, Andy said, "You'll never guess… but I got an email from Cynthia Collins about a month ago. She didn't say much. Just that she's been working for Crane Analytical for almost a year and she's got a promotion. She seems to like her work, but doesn't say much about what's going on other than that."

"She was always quite the loner," commented Mariah. "I never really seemed to be able to connect with her. She worked for Rathburn. I wonder how much she ever really knew about what he was up to?"

Andy contemplated what he knew about Cynthia's involvement with Rathburn, but decided that it could remain unsaid. Instead, he said, "In the end, it was Cynthia who gave us the clue where we could find Lisa. I will always be grateful to her for that." Andy looked over to Lisa, who nodded her agreement.

"Speaking of Rathburn," Kayla broke in, "he's gone. When we went up to Hayward to see my folks last week, we went on up to Superior and stopped by campus. There is a new professor in Rathburn's office, new name on the door, what was it?" she looked at Gary, "Whittinger, Whittington,… something like that."

"Yeah," agreed Gary. "And we saw Jodi and Jamie. They are both due to graduate in a week or so. Jodi is looking good. You'd never know she'd been in that accident."

"Oh, and we've got to tell you," Kayla grinned. "If you need a used car, Peter Dahle is running a used car lot on Garfield Avenue in Duluth."

"Really?" Andy asked.

"Yeah. 'Dahle's Used Cars' it says on a big sign out front. We didn't stop in to say hi or anything, but we're pretty sure it's him. We did notice this big head shop right across the street. It's a very strange neighborhood."

"Well, you have to start somewhere, I guess," mused Mariah. "Maybe he's found his business gimmick?"

The students relived their memories of Burlington until Gary and Kayla had to leave. After they said their goodbyes, Mariah retired to her room while Andy and Lisa put the leftovers in the fridge, loaded the dishwasher and cleaned up the kitchen.

"Let's go sit a minute," suggested Andy. It was dark outside, and the room was illuminated only by the gaudy chandelier that had been turned down to a soft yellow glow. They reclined at one end of the couch with Lisa leaning her head on Andy's shoulder. "That was a fun dinner, wasn't it?" he asked.

"Yeah," agreed Lisa lazily. She pulled the scrunchie from her ponytail and let her hair cascade over her shoulders. Playing idly with the scrunchie she mused, "Can you imagine Kayla and Gary starting a family?"

Andy thought for a moment and then said, "Yeah, I can. I bet that they will be good parents."

"Hmmm…" agreed Lisa.

"Can you imagine us starting a family?" asked Andy.

Lisa roused a little from her relaxed position. "Well, yes, actually I can." She thought for a moment. Turning to look up at Andy, "I think that I would like that a lot, but right now I don't want to give up what I'm doing. Is that okay?"

Andy smiled and nodded. "Yeah, I think that is just fine, and I'm with you all the way."

Lisa settled back against Andy's shoulder and snuggled into his arms.

"If we had a baby," mused Andy presently, "I bet he'd be really smart like you."

"Hah," responded Lisa, "if we had a baby, I bet she'd be strong and kind like you."

The two lay in each other's arms for a moment. Lisa tilted her head to look up at Andy. "We should stay in practice though, don't you think?"

Andy chuckled and tilted Lisa's face up to his and kissed her. "Absolutely, yes," he replied.

Acknowledgements

The author wishes to thank his wife and friends who have been so supportive during the writing of this work. Specific thanks go out to Suzanne Hagen, Becky Kleager, Bill Rasmussen, Marshall Toman and Ruth Wood for their helpful comments.

Biography

David B. Rusterholz is a retired professor of organic chemistry living in western Wisconsin. In his spare time, he enjoys woodworking and maintaining his mineral collection.